NINJA NANNY

BY NATALIE NEWPORT

<u>Reviews of *Ninja Nanny*</u>:

After reading this book: you will never ever want to be a nanny, but you will want to be a ninja! Ninja Nanny is non-stop adventure and pure awesomeness.
-Christian Mollitor, author of *Chimneys: a ghost story*

Join Natalie Newport, aka the Ninja Nanny, as she discovers her hidden talents and superpowers, and falls in love. You'll likely fall in love with her in the process.
–Rebecca Shupe, Author of
Choosing Your Harmony: Embracing This Journey We Call Life

This book is all about being faced with challenges (hurdles) and overcoming (jumping) them. It appeals to the inner ninja in us all.
–Brett Clay, Author of *Selling Change*

Inside this delicious book, you will find firefighters, talking cats, and absolute mayhem...but it all leads to a place of tranquility.
– Frank Reed , Author of *In God We Trust: Dollars & Sense*

Somehow, I can sleep more soundly at night, knowing Ninja Nanny is out there, fighting the good fight.
–James Donaldson, author of *Standing Above the Crowd*

Convertible sports cars, firefighter conventions, talking cats, precocious children, and, of course, caffeine. What more could a reader want?
–BJ Farish, author of *Shattering Your Barriers*

Holy Shinobi! Newport stealthily and artfully ambushes the reader into recalling and reliving life's sometimes awkward, resonating and always identifiable universal moments. Small town girl or highly skilled practitioner of ancient craft—either way, this tale is pure omiyage!
–Giovanna Mosca Franklin

Ninja Nanny

忍者ナニー

NATALIE NEWPORT

SYNCLECTIC MEDIA

Published by **Synclectic Media**
Seattle, Washington
www.synclectic.com

Publisher's Cataloging-in-Publication Data

Newport, Natalie
  Ninja Nanny / Natalie Newport. – 2nd ed.
    p. cm. –
  Summary: Natalie Newport has always prided herself on having her stuff together. She has led the perfect double-edged, double life: Nanny by day, and Ninja by night. But now Natalie's in bit of a pickle. Everything's changing at once: She's just graduated high school and the family she works for invited her to move with them to Europe. Also, Natalie is completely enamored with a firefighter who works out at her gym, and wants to find out if he likes her—which will be tough, since she has only ever taken calculated risks in the past. She starts having mystical visions and her cats start speaking to her. Just when Natalie starts wondering if she's losing it, her trainer tells her she has superpowers. What's going on with the Ninja Nanny?
  Library of Congress Control Number: 2011938078
  ISBN: 978-0615535654
  [1. Action & Adventure—Fiction. 2. Romance—Fiction. 3. Coming of Age—Fiction.] I. Title.
PS3613.E97   2011938078
[Fic]—813.6N   p-CIP

---

10 9 8 7 6 5 4 3 2 1

Ω
Second Edition
Printed in the United States

Dedicated:

To those who have stuck with me through it all.
You know who you are, and that
I love you.

Peace, love &
roundhouse kicks !

Ninja
Nanny

**NORTHWEST
BURN
FOUNDATION**

10% of the publisher's proceeds from
Ninja Nanny will be donated to
Northwest Burn Foundation.

Empty your mind,
be formless…
shapeless, like water.
If you put water into a cup, it becomes the cup.
You put water into a bottle; it becomes the bottle.
You put it into a teapot; it becomes the teapot.
Water can flow, or it can crash.
Be water, my friend…

Bruce Lee

The Big Day

I had looked forward to this day for what seemed like eons. I'd practiced for it for same. I was to face an actual ninja in the secret dojo underneath the gym where I worked out! I practiced my jabs, upper cuts and back fists, preparing for what was to come, and then moving on to kicks.

This was the first time I'd dressed all in black to spar. I was nervous as hell, but vowed not to show it. We were allowed to use hands and feet only, no weapons. There was only one rule: I was to disable my opponent by any means necessary, but if either of us got seriously injured, we had to stop.

I didn't know which direction he, or she, would be coming from. There were mirrors everywhere and four entryways, sans doors. I stood in the center of the room, waiting, breathing, grounding and centering. I imagined the strength of the planet coming up through the earth and floor into my feet to assist me and give me power, balance and stamina. I self-checked, making sure I was alert but not stiff. I had to keep flexible and loose, ready for anything.

It was official. I was in *the zone.*

I sensed a movement behind me and to the right. I turned and saw a fast flash of black coming straight at me, instantly aware that the flash was male and unarmed. I remembered the helpful hints my trainer had given me: *Use your intuition.* I sensed my opponent's fierceness; that he was quick to act and wanted to get the job done—the job of defeating his opponent. Maybe too quick.

…Don't give away your moves.

So to that end I let him come at me, waiting to see what he'd do before I responded. He was so fast, his wiry body whirring with energy—almost too fast to see. Almost like the Tasmanian Devil from cartoons. Suddenly, he did a roundhouse kick. I ducked to avoid it, looked up and he had disappeared.

I was no longer in the dojo, but in the mountains, in Japan. I realized that I now had the body I'd had as a child when I lived there.

I remembered this place. My parents had taken me here the day I turned 5. It was a special birthday trip, to enjoy nature and each other.

As we started the drive home after a fun day of sightseeing and hiking, I saw a summer camp of boys practicing martial arts outside. There were about a hundred, all sparring in pairs, and all evenly spaced in the field. I was mesmerized. I asked my parents if I could learn. They said no, I was a girl and should focus on other sports, like tennis or track. I knew this was a typical protective parent response, but I wasn't upset. I knew I would learn someday.

And then I saw him.

I knew his face instantly, but wasn't sure from where. I waved and he waved back. My parents drove on, unnoticing.

When I came to, I was sweating, and remembered nothing of the fight. My opponent shook my hand in ninja fashion, quickly and without feeling, and left through the door kitty corner to the one he'd entered from.

As Jin congratulated and hugged me, I looked into the face of the man I'd waved at as a child, realizing I'd always known this face. He smiled for a split second, some combination of recognition and humor playing across his face. His brown eyes flashed a deep green for a moment, and I thought I was seeing things.

"Phoenix, we should talk. However, I teach a class in 10 minutes."

"Okay, I understand. See you next session."

We bowed to each other, and he silently left the room.

Life inside the training studio was usually pretty simple. I was given challenges and met them head on. It was a lot of hard work, but there were very few surprises. The outcome was for the most part known. Either one opponent would win, or the other would. The benefits of training were also known, of course. Being in excellent physical shape speaks for itself. There was no clutter here, which made it easy to think clearly. The only humans I laid eyes on were those who'd been invited—one could enter this dojo by special invitation only.

Life outside the studio: not so simple. I didn't have an instructor or training manual for how to deal with this guy I had my eye on, who seemed shy and wouldn't make a move.

Well, to be honest, I didn't just like him—he totally consumed my thoughts. The crush was out of control, and needed to be dealt with. Only…I didn't want to deal. For the first time in my life, I wanted to run away. I was scared of everything, rejection, or worse. The possibility he might actually like me back. I didn't know which was scarier. I could face adversaries as I'd learned to do in training, but not this flippin' firefighter.

Children, Conundrums & Change

Outside the studio, before the firefighter showed up in my life, I had everything under control. I felt good about my life as a nanny. My finances were in order, and life was just peachy keen, jelly bean.

I knew I could make a decent income as a nanny, and could learn a lot about how to take care of kids. That's exactly what I'd been doing for 2 years. Cleaning, learning and earning. I wanted a solid foundation for my life, and stability. I wasn't good at dealing with change. Little did I know, however, changes were blowing in with the breeze: *big* changes.

I was conceived and born in Japan, and spent the first five years of my life there. I was fascinated by martial arts, but my parents wouldn't let me learn them, saying they were too dangerous. Even then, I remember thinking that not learning them would be more dangerous. But try explaining that in five-year-old language. We moved to Washington State, but I never forgot the early days and ways, and I yearned to go back.

I was born to be bad. I had a fire in me that just wouldn't let me settle down and live a normal life (whatever that might be). Plus, my nanny job was with a newborn. All the softness and cuddling and baby faces and baby talk just about made me want to puke. It was an easy job, because that baby couldn't backtalk or throw tantrums—he just cried, and 9 times out of 10, I plugged him up with the pacifier. It worked. Those tenth times were rough, but rare. Such a good baby.

One has to find balance in life. This nannying job didn't put out my fire, so I started taking martial arts lessons. I took them for a year, and I got good. I took them for two, and I got even better.

My schedule looked like this:

7:30am-5:30pm:

Super loving, nurturing, sweet, gentle,
controlled substitute mom

7:30pm-9:30pm:

Operation Ninja

Those last two hours of my day taught me how to toughen up, be strong, and hone those reflexes. In essence, they taught me how to be a fighter. They felt very clandestine, as they were held in the basement of my gym. Only martial artists knew about the place. This included the gym's owner, Jin, who kept his skills a secret. Since I learned both Japanese and Chinese forms, I referred to Jin as both

Sensei and Sifu. Being a business owner, he had to keep a lot of things secret.

So I was feeling fairly decent about life, in general. I had a chance to convince this firefighter he couldn't live without me. I would keep the training quiet, and what he didn't know wouldn't hurt his pride. He could remain feeling like Mr. Studly without ever knowing my secret.

Then my world was turned upside down. The proverbial carpet was pulled out from under me. The tablecloth was pulled from the table, like in that magic trick where all the dishes stay put, but this time—they all broke. Dark clouds gathered, a heavy rain pelted down, and lightning bolts made the sidewalks hiss all around me, and the question hung in the air: "How would Natalie, the nefarious Ninja Nanny find someone to help her quell the fires within? How on earth would she ever find love now?"

Shake It, Cali

The family I worked for the last two years, since I turned 16 and legally able to work, was moving away. Not just away, but overseas to Italy, their next station, far from beautiful, soggy Washington state, the families they'd gotten to know, and me. They had asked me to accompany them as an au pair.

I could imagine becoming fluent in Italian, wearing Versace every day, and bumping into George Clooney at Lake Como. I imagined saying goodbye to my boring, predictable lifestyle to hobnob with George and his buddies, the rich, the famous, the carefree. Julia Roberts might suddenly need a nanny for her kids, and I'd be there, at the ready. How convenient—I could still have my own spending money, but of course not have time or need to spend it. George and I would make excellent use of weekends to enjoy trips to the Riviera. We would frequent film festivals and travel by his billion-dollar yacht all over Europe. People in the biz would notice my natural dark red hair, the faraway look in my mysterious eyes, and I'd land a film deal.

Alas, I had just signed a lease on a new apartment, and didn't want to pay a bunch of money to break it. The last time I did that, I had to pay the remainder of the year's rent, as if I were living there. Not nice for Natalie.

Hmm...Hollywood, Europe, George, Julia, exotic clothes, jewelry, food, sights...or the comforts of home.

(Insert long, thoughtful pause, in
elegant, graceful thinking pose.)

Well, even though I didn't like being left, I ended up staying put.

I found a new family with two seemingly delightful kids, aged two and three. The parents, Camalia and Carl, seemed very sweet and liked me. I took the job. However, after my most recent stint of nannyhood (with the only vacations being major American holidays) I was a girl in need of a retreat before settling into the new job with the new family.

Then again, I was also in desperate need of a break from thinking about this guy— the firefighter— who worked out at my gym. He had wavy, chestnut hair, the most sincere blue eyes I'd ever seen, and big hands. Hands that could hold a woman and make her feel safe. Hands that could cup certain parts of the body, and fingers that would...

Ooofda! My hand hit my forehead, which had suddenly started to perspire like crazy. Major hot flashes just thinking of this man. I had to stop for a second, I felt faint. Breathe, Natalie, just breathe. Breathing is the secret to life, like in Castaway, where Tom Hanks is stuck on that island alone. In, out. Innnn, oooout.

Okay. Now that I'd composed myself, I could go on. See what thinking about this guy did to me?! It made me into a big mass of quivering jelly inside. I never showed it at the gym, though. I couldn't. I didn't want his ego to inflate into a huge balloon and float him away into the sky. Plus, I was a rebel. I had a rep to protect. I told myself not to tell anyone that he was my real reason for staying, but he was. I could give a flip about the apartment—this family paid me enough to rent two apartments, and still live comfortably. It was all about the firefighter.

His name? Hammer. That's a codename. We all had codenames, even me. When I discussed the people in my life, I always used their codenames. I had my own rules about things, but this was part of the Chi Club's (our little martial arts club) covert operations. One couldn't be overheard plotting a strategy with one's instructor or classmates, so one had to use code. It was a rule established and instated to keep everyone safe. As a Ninja, my codename was Phoenix.

But back to men: one of my personal rules was that every male would start out with positive points—meaning, if he messed up, he would be docked a certain number of points. Points could be made up, but it'd take a lot. A whole hell of a lot: groveling, gifts—the jewelry type, chocolate, flowers, and massages.

In a perfect world, every male would remain glowingly positive in the points department. They'd be the wonderful creatures they could be—honest, helpful, affectionate, sensitive, passionate at the right times, and they'd know when to leave us alone to go out with the girls and take a night out with the guys.

In this world, unfortunately, hardly any males—at least the ones I knew—had any points left. They either lingered right around zero, or were tragically in the negative. The dismal numbers from my personal dating history, coupled with my crush on a firefighter, who would probably not be cool with dating a martial artist, meant one thing: vacation.

Vacation: now. Not after six months, or a year of nannying, but right freaking now. I needed out of the county, and out of the state. Far enough away from things to think, but not far enough that I'd never see him again. "Where my girls at?" I thought, and I immediately called Sam.

Sam was my best friend. She was curvy, sassy as all hell, and most importantly, she was there for me. She'd saved the money from a tax refund and was going down to California to visit a friend who was getting married later in the year. She was down with the plan. Don't you just love how things work out so smoothly sometimes? (Believe me; in my life when that happens, it's the calm before the storm. Life is trying to prepare me for a blow by sucking in its breath for a good two days first and then letting loose like a kid does on birthday candles.) We decided we'd go the next weekend. I started my job in two weeks, so we could take a few more days if we wanted, lollygag and hit the beach with the bride-to-be. Remember what they say about those best-laid plans?

We hit the road on Friday afternoon. She drove her car to SeaTac instead of hitting I-5 South and I had no idea why. I looked over at the side of her face. It looked mischievous.

"Uh oh. What is that look on your face?"

"Nothing," she answered, dimple flashing and eyes twinkling.

"Huh. So here we are at SeaTac Airport and Natalie has no idea why."

"Right you are."

"Girl, what are you up to?"

Still no answer.

"Will we be flying today?" Just a closed mouthed smile this time, and a little giggle. "Alright, just wait 'til your birthday comes and see what Natalie has in store for you."

This got a response. She pulled into a parking space. "I just wanted to stop driving so I could explain it to you," she said, unconvincingly. I'll admit, a little mystery can be a good thing, so I was enjoying how she set up the suspense.

"Scared of the birthday surprise, huh?" I stifled an evil chuckle.

"Natalie, I rented a car," she explained with utmost composure, ignoring my question. "I thought we should ride in style, before you give up your freedom for another year."

My eyes welled up. Yes, my sentence was to be a year. Minimum. Another year of nannydom, when I'd had such high hopes of being a famous... or something, by now.

What a true friend Sam was to me. I found it rare to come across such a genuine soul, who would do cool things like rent a convertible just because she knew you needed it. Well, and because her friend from Chico happened to be getting married (and Sam was going to be in the wedding, so there were preparations to be made).

We walked to the counter at the car rental place, she signed the paperwork, and got the keys, toting our bags to the parking space they'd told us about, and vavaVOOM! It was a Mitsubishi Spyder—new, and silver. We stood and sighed in unison.

I touched it. I whimpered. She laughed, a little crazily. She didn't know it would be this nice. I opened the doors and took a whiff of that 'new car' smell. "Ahh yeah, baby, that's what I'm talkin' about!"

"And because you are all that you are, I'll let you drive first."

Doh! What more could a girl ask for in life? At that moment, not much.

We sat there, pushing buttons and exploring. We found the convertible button and pushed it. The roof retracted and we sighed in unison, sitting in awe for another moment. I started up this beautiful little silver pimpmobile, both giggling uncontrollably, and I pulled out, and wound down, around and around the spiral SeaTac exit. I felt a rumble in my soul, which materialized in the pit of my stomach and crystallized into words in my throat.

"My name is Natalie and this is how I roll! Yeeeeaaaaaahhhhhhhhhhhhhhhhhhh!" My words and Sam's laughter echoed down the ramp as we revved off into the great unknown, her long dark hair and my long red hair flying in the wind.

I had burned a couple CD's with all these driving songs on them. Currently, we were cruising down the freeway in the hot, hot sun, jamming out to Dave Matthews. Sam was now driving; she looked over at me and thanked me for creating Road Trip Tunes Volumes I & II. I said, "No problem." Then I told her we needed some of those scarves for our hair like Thelma and Louise, not including the part about dying at the end, of course, and asked if we could stop and get some. She smiled, mischievously again, pulled the car over, and popped the trunk.

"I've been saving these since ninth grade," she said.

"For what?"

"Honestly, I didn't know until right now." She pulled one gold and one black scarf out.

"I love this woman!" I shouted, just like on that jewelry commercial where the husband embarrassed his wife, but without the romantic undertones, of course. People looked and laughed along with us.

"Which one would you like?"

I gave her a look that said surely you jest.

She caught it. "Oh. Dumb question." She handed over the black one.

We had arrived at a bookstore in Oregon, and went in to use the facilities and get something to eat. While munching, we went over the itinerary.

It looked something like this:

1. Arrive destination #1: Chico, CA.
2. Gallivant around for a while, see some sights.
3. Find cheap place to crash. Crash.
4. After a couple days, take trip to coast w/bride-to-be.
5. Drive on beach at high speed like Jack Nicholson and Shirley MacLaine in Terms of Endearment, without anyone being catapulted into the water, of course.
6. Stay in Chico for as short a time as possible because we want to see—
7. Destinations #2 & 3: the Redwoods and the coast.
8. If we get adventurous, head to Monterey; otherwise just take our time meandering home.

That was as much as we'd planned out. A couple freewheeling chicks like us thought the following about too much planning: *Eww.*

After a couple more pit stops and a few Kodak moment stops, we headed through the mountains at sunset. The natural scenery was stunning. At one point, these guys tried to flirt with us at a restroom somewhere, but they were more interested in the car than us, or at least it seemed that way, and we were more interested in the car than in them, so we took off with Sam at the wheel.

I woke up alone in the car, in a motel parking lot. Sam came back and informed me we were in Chico. Again, she had a mysterious look on her face.

"What's up?"

"Umm…." She said, starting to giggle.

"What, what?"

"There's a firefighter convention in town."

"Ahem." I took a moment, rubbed my eyes. "What did you say?"

She slowed her speech. "A *convention* of firefighters. Right here, Chico, California. This weekend."

"You better be blowing smoke up my you-know-what."

"Not only am I not blowing smoke up there, but there's no vacancy!"

"…" I gestured around the town, doing a swirling motion with my hands.

"Anywhere."

"Oh, cripes. Flying balls of flubber. You're serious, aren't you?"

"Yes." She looked at me with one of her contemplative I know what the Universe is trying to tell you gazes. Then we both had to laugh. Hard.

"Well, I feel better," I said. She just looked at me.

"I know, I know, it doesn't change the facts. I need to do something about this crush."

"Fo sho."

"All right, thanks for your helpful advice. You know my brain is scrambled every time I start to think about him."

"Yeah, I know. I'll stop toying needlessly with your emotions, but that'll be tomorrow morning after I've had a shower and a good night's sleep."

"That's fair. I could use the same. Where are we to get clean and rested though?"

"Yeah, about Plan B. Since my friend is out of town for another night, and I don't have the key..."

"We're screwed."

"Pretty much."

"Flip."

"Your swear words don't quite cut it for delivery."

"Sorry, I'll try harder next time. It's just, I'm aware we have an audience."

"What are we, PG? Can't we at least be rated PG 13?"

"I'm serious, Sam, we're being watched," I whispered.

"For real? From where?"

"Yeah. There's someone watching us from that window."

Sam and I looked over in the direction of the window in question. The curtain moved, and then it was still. Silence.

"Well, I wonder who just heard our convers—"

Just then, the door opened, and a guy about our age came out. We watched, cautiously, curiously, as he approached. "Good evening, ladies."

"Hello," Sam and I said in unison. The gentleman stepped into the light, and I tried to hide that I was noticing the tan, muscular arms, attached to the broad chest, attached to broad shoulders and strong neck, attached to a head with dark hair and blue eyes that were both warm and penetrating. Yowza!

"I couldn't help overhearing..."

"Oh! Sorry if we woke you," I said, staring at his bulging biceps.

"No, not at all." He stifled a smile. "I heard you didn't have a place to stay."

"Well, that's true..." Sam hesitated, ever the careful one, not to tell too much to a stranger.

"We just drove here from Washington State, we're exhausted, smelly, and pissed off," I blurted.

"All right," he said, processing. "I understand the exhausted and smelly, but pissed off...?"

"That there happens to be a firefighter convention in Chico and they happen to be taking up every room in the whole flippin' town!" I continued, fuming.

Again, he stifled a smile. "Well, yes, there is a convention. We have them every year. Didn't you know about it?"

This time it was Sam's turn to fume, just a little. "I grew up here, and no, I didn't know about it," she said.

"Ah. Well, we've only been having them for five years. It's one of the rare times all the rooms in Chico are used up."

"You don't say," Sam said sarcastically. She was rarely sarcastic. I knew she must've been bone tired.

"Listen, mister..."

"Malone. Mickey Malone." Sam and I looked at each other—is this guy for real? He caught the glance. "My dad was a baseball player. He chose names for all his kids that sounded like they could be baseball star names."

"Did any of the kids end up baseball stars?"

"Two girls and four boys later, no. Dog trainer, accountant, firefighter, firefighter, teacher, and the youngest just went into the navy."

"Wait, you said firefighter twice," I said, ever the observant one.

"Yeah. My younger brother is a firefighter too. He's staying across the way," he said, pointing across the parking lot.

"You've got to be kidding." I turned to Sam. "Are we on Candid Camera? Are all our friends going to come out from behind the bushes now and yell that we've been Punked, and laugh and bring cake, tunes, balloons, and turn this into a big party?"

"No," Sam said, "But it certainly does feel that surreal." She took a deep breath. "Listen, it's late. I have to meet an old friend tomorrow and be fitted for a bridesmaid's dress. Tomorrow night is the rehearsal dinner, and I don't want to greet everyone with bags under my eyes. Mickey, are you going to offer us a place to stay or what?"

I was shocked that Sam, the careful one, would be so forward, but when it came to sleep, this girl did not mess around.

"Yeah. Actually, there are two beds in each room. I know my brother is still awake, because I noticed his TV on just a few minutes ago," he said, pointing to a window across the way.

"Oh, you mean when you were spying on us?" I said.

This time his grin was full, not stifled. "Well, your conversation came right through my window. I noticed two ladies in a bit of a pickle and firefighters are trained to help in any and all situations," he countered.

"Fair enough," I said. Boy, did this one know how to turn on the charm, and when he did, irresistible. I hoped he'd saved some of the good genes for his little brother.

"I'll go knock on his door and tell him what's up," Mickey said, striding across the parking lot.

"Take your time," I said, waving and smiling.

I turned to Sam. "What are we going to do? Are you down with this plan? If so, which brother do you want?

They could be murderers for all we know!" My voice was a high pitched, nervous whisper.

"Calm down. Yeah, I'm down with this plan. At least this way we'll get showers out of the deal, instead of having to sleep cramped up in that." We looked at the Spyder. Hmm. Nice, but not good car camping. "And yes, they could be axe murderers, but I put my vibe on it, and I'm certain they're simply California firefighters."

"Okay." I trusted Sam's vibe like no other. "I thought you'd be thinking of what your mother might say, but if you're not, great."

"I'm far too exhausted to consider Mom at this point. Plus if anything happens, my cell is on."

"Yeah, me too. So…which brother did you want, again?"

"Well, why don't we wait and—"

Just then, Mickey sauntered up behind us with a younger version of himself. This one had warm brown eyes, was a little tanner and not quite as muscular, but still toned. "Hi," he said, extending a hand to Sam first. "Marty."

I saw Sam's eyes light up for just a brief second, like I had never seen before, and then she masked it. The guys didn't catch it, but I did. I know my friend. "Sam," she said, giving a shy-but-still flirtatious smile. I saw Marty relax, just slightly. They were already melting into each other.

"Well, I guess that answers that question," I said.

"Which question?" asked Mickey.

"Oh, nothing," I said, grinning mischievously.

"Shall we?" Mickey said.

"We shall," I replied, giving Sam a quick hug and following him inside. "You must have a huge day ahead tomorrow at the convention. What do firefighters do at firefighter conventions, anyway?"

And with that, Sam and Marty went to his room, and that's the last I saw of them until morning. Until I'd caught their eyes light up, I'd been thinking of asking the brothers to sleep in one room and let us have the other. But obviously, they had their reasons for wanting to sleep separately. And I had mine.

Signs & More Signs

I awoke to the sound of soft, fast knocking at the door. I peeped through the hole at the maid standing there, so I opened it, smiled with squinty morning eyes, and asked her to come back later. I looked at the bedside clock, and it was 6:45am. What on earth was the cleaning lady doing knocking so early?

"Actually, we requested that someone wake us early. The festivities get started at 8:30am, so we have to clean up, and start our 6,000 calorie day. I thought we'd get a wakeup call, but I guess they prefer the personal touch."

"I guess they do. Hold it, wait. How many calories did you say?"

"6,000. On average. To put back what we burn off. There's a lot more to it, of course, but that's a rough average. And just when we're working, obviously."

"That's so wrong. You guys can eat that much and look that good. I'm in the wrong business, apparently."

"What business are you in, Ms. Natalie?"

"The nanny business."

"Ah, I see. So you run around chasing little brats all day?"

"Well, not really. I mean, I didn't, at my old job, just took care of a baby."

"And that one ended?"

"Yeah…the family moved to Europe."

"So now what are you doing?"

I told him the story of how I'd gotten this new nanny job. He sat, contemplated it for a moment, and blew out a big breath of air. "They're how old?"

"Two and three."

"The boy being the oldest?"

"Yep."

"You have your work cut out for you."

"Yeah, but I can handle anything." After all, I was Ninja Nanny.

"I wish you luck," and with that, he gave me a kiss on the forehead and headed into the commode.

Mentally, I recounted the details of the evening. I'd gotten dressed for bed in some pointedly non-sexy pajamas, consisting of workout shorts and a sleeveless shirt. As I exited the bathroom, Mickey was already lying in bed. His bed. Reclined back, hands clasped behind his head, elbows out, shirt off, eyes closed. Drool. Hearing me, his eyes opened and cut to me. I quickly looked away and started heading towards my bed.

"Whoa," he said.

"What?"

"Where'd you get such amazing biceps?"

"Oh, you know, I picked them up at the local bicep shop."

"Very funny. But I'm serious. Yours rival mine, and for a girl…"

"Yeah yeah, for a girl…"

"Take it as a compliment. So how often do you workout, and for how long?"

"Every day. And how long have I been working out, or how long each time do I workout?"

"Both."

"I have been working out for two years straight. Before that, I waffled, and now I'm more…religious about it. Every other day I do two hours, in between, I do one. Best not to kill oneself, right?"

"Well, I'm impressed."

"Thank you. I'm still working on the areas that jiggle, which seem a lot harder to get rid of…"

"Where? I don't see any." Now, he was grinning.

"Are you patronizing me?"

"Not at all. Just admiring what I see. Plus, guys like a little more in certain areas. Gives us something to hold onto."

"Are you trying to seduce me with your words?"

"If I were, what would you say?"

"Well…"

Right in the middle of my reverie, Sam came in. She had that same mischievous half-smile on her face. She glanced over at Mickey, who was snoring lightly.

"Good morning," I said. It was a loaded "good morning," the type of greeting that said, tell me all right now or *die*. We slid outside the door and grinned at each other like little girls sharing a secret on a playground.

"I think it's a love connection," she said through a giggle.

"WHAT?!?" I jumped up off the bed and hugged her. "Right on, girl! Congratulations." Sam had closed herself off from the world for a while—too long a while, in my opinion. I couldn't have been more thrilled.

"We talked for like two hours. It was weird... I never expected to have such a connection with a firefighter; I mean, I work at a bank! But we connected. And he kissed me, and it was obvious from the kiss..."

"That something was there."

"Exactly. This morning, I awoke to him stroking my hair. This was very... unexpected and..." I could see she was getting emotional. "...sweet."

I looked into her eyes. "Oh, Sam! You really like him."

"I wasn't expecting to, but...yeah." I hugged her again.

"Now tell me all about your time. We have like five seconds, so give me the low down, dirty scoop right now and hurry up about it."

"Um, well, I don't know if right now would be the best time. Nothing really happened and we've been eavesdropped on by a firefighter before."

She just looked at me, not buying this excuse. "You're kidding. Nothing happened?"

"Well, you see, it's like this..."

At that precise moment, the drapes came open, and a firefighter in boxer briefs with a 6-pack stood there, smiling out at us, "Nothing happened, Sam. Good morning."

"Uh, um, g'morning," Sam sputtered. I didn't know if this was from being embarrassed at being caught in the middle of a conversation about Mickey and Marty, or from seeing Mickey in just his boxers, but I guessed it was a combination of both.

"Well," Mickey said, pulling on a shirt, "I guess I'll go see how Marty's doing waking up. Sounds like he didn't get all that much sleep, so he'll probably need a little help."

Sam blushed for the first time (or the first time in front of me anyway). There were many firsts going on these days for her. "Um, I'll go with you."

"Suit yourself," Mickey said.

"Well, as long as you two are going, I'll come too. If there's breakfast involved, I'm there. Even in PJ's."

So we all promenaded across the parking lot in our pajamas, for everyone awake at this bright, ungodly hour to observe. As we entered the room, the very perceptible sound of Marty's snoring reached my ears. I saw Mickey glance at the other bed (as yet still made) and go to the far side of Marty's bed.

He tickled the back of Marty's neck. Marty giggled. He grabbed a piece of the sheet and started playing with Marty's ear. Marty growled, and said "Come to bed, you fiery vixen." At this, Sam and I were on the floor in stitches. Mickey blew on his brother's shoulder, and Marty rolled over, intending to grab Sam to roll her into bed with him. At the last minute, his eyes opened and he yelled out in shock. And then the whole thing turned into a display of roughhousing, all in the name of brotherly love.

Sam and I snuck out, giggling. "Well, at least we know their family knows how to show affection," I said.

"Yeah, ha ha. So really, nothing happened between you and Mickey?"

I looked back to see their door still shut. "He heard the part of our conversation last night, about me having to get over this damn firefighter."

"Oh. Sorry." Sam cringed.

"No, it's okay. I got a sample. He was willing to sacrifice himself for the good cause of me getting over a fellow firefighter."

"Hey, what a guy," Sam said. "This must be some kind of firefighter allegiance. He was willing to take one for the team."

"Yeah, ha ha. Well, I tried. His arms felt very big and strong, and I felt safe and very...warm. But there was no heat."

"I...think I know what you mean," Sam said.

"No spark, no chemistry beyond the initial excitement of being with somebody new. He is amazing. He's just not..."

"Hammer?"

"Yeah. It's not like I can just sleep with a firefighter and be cured of this. I need him, and only him. Or if he doesn't feel the same, I at least need to resolve things with him before I move on."

"Yes but there are other guys you'll have chemistry with, don'tcha think?"

"Yeah, but..."

"Okay, I get it. Your heart has gotten involved with Hammer."

"Precisely. It's not just chemistry, which in itself is elusive, in life. It's that feeling of deep friendship, like you'd do absolutely anything for that person, without question."

"Got it. So now, tell me what happened. You said you tried, with Mickey. What does that mean?"

"Well, we were flirting, innocently, noticing each other's muscles. And that led to him asking about who else notices mine, which led to a discussion about Hammer. He admitted hearing that part of your and my conversation, then, and being such an understanding, empathetic soul, offered himself up as a sacrifice, in the name of me getting the heck over it."

"And then?"

"He said he has a girlfriend, just started dating her but nothing in common, no bond, and she lives in another town so he doesn't see it lasting."

"And?"

"…Invited me over. To his bed."

"Yes, then what transpired? Get to the point, girl, I'm dying in suspense, here."

"We were lying on our sides. He said my name. He grabbed my hand and pulled me against him. I could feel his excitement. He didn't try to shove his tongue in my mouth right away, which was nice. He eased into it, and he wasn't all hands, either: a gentleman."

"So you weren't turned on at all?"

"That's just it! My body was, but my head was all over the map. I didn't know the person I was kissing and that was just weird. I mean, I had that experience senior year, but it was after being at a party for hours and I did know the guy from school. The couple times I didn't, I was so wasted I didn't remember anything. I was a wild girl back then, Sam. Wild in deed, on occasion, but not in thought. I always wanted love, a constant, a safe harbor in the storm of life. Back then, because love didn't present itself, I was willing to…experiment more, and none of those experiments turned to love. That was a good lesson, not starting relationships with sex. Anyway, I'm still the same girl. But I don't want or need a bunch of one-night stands to tell me what I already know: that I'm in love with Hammer, and no one else measures up."

"I hear you. We do have to kiss lot of frogs to find the prince, don't we?" Sam said knowingly.

"Yeah, we sure do." I sighed.

"I guess I missed out on those senior year party experiences, because the last time I seriously dated was a few years ago," Sam said.

"Yeah, I get that. You are making up for lost time. I am so thrilled for you, too, and that's for real."

"In a way, I envy you," Sam said, eyes meeting mine. "You didn't deny what was happening in life, so you've evolved and you're right where you should be."

I rubbed my temples, still getting used to the bright morning sun. "Yeah well, that somehow doesn't make where I'm at right now any easier. How come it can't be more like it is on nature shows?"

Sam looked at me quizzically, so I explained myself. "For instance, there are these crabs in Cuba. They live in the forest, but spawn in the ocean. So they make the trip, slip into the water, and jump up and down until the eggs are all gone. They put salsa music to accompany this ritual, which makes it look like they're dancing."

"I get it. They eat, mate, give birth, dance, and enjoy life."

"Exactly. Without all the thinking, planning, analyzing. They live on a tropical island where it's hot and beautiful. They find shade to rest in the heat of the day so they don't dehydrate on their trip. The only problem is, some of them get crunched by car tires on the way back to the woods. But they do have a fighting chance, and at least it's quick when they die. Crunch, it's over. They did what they were meant to do, with a sense of community, and the strength of power in numbers. They can feel good about the babies they released into the sea."

"You're right. We could learn a lot from watching Animal Planet more often. But you'll get through this somehow. I know how strong you are."

I loved how staggeringly much she believed in me.

I hugged her and laughed. "Well, I don't know how many firefighter conventions I can handle without going nutty," I said.

After saying goodbye to the guys and showering, we made our way to a coffee stand, and were then able to think clearly about where to eat breakfast. After taking care of that important business, we drove to Sam's friend Abby's apartment where she lived with her 12-year-old son. We actually made it to the bride's house that morning without any fires or fire trucks in sight.

Immediately, I liked the kid, who said his mom was in the shower. He reminded me of everything I loved about kids, and I suddenly felt better about my upcoming job. He saw the car and his eyes got really wide. He asked Sam if he could drive, adding that he'd been driving for two years on back roads, and she said no. But there was that twinkle in her eyes that said "Maybe, when your mom's not around." He caught the look, shut up and just smiled silently, like a Cheshire cat.

I met Abby. I liked her too. Soon though, the discussion turned into wedding plans, in which I had no interest (except for my own wedding or that of a close friend). I also had no knowledge of weddings, since I had only ever been in one, that of a good friend from high school. It involved showing up, getting pretty, watching the wedding, and partying until the break of dawn—my kind of wedding. I had always hoped that Sam would meet, like at the end of My Best Friend's Wedding, a debonair, handsome gentleman who would swirl her around the dance floor (except he wouldn't actually prefer men like the character from the film, so she could truly have her Hollywood ending ☺).

Leaving Sam and company to wedding plans, I swam a few laps in the pool outside. Feeling refreshed, I decided to go for a walk. I giggled to myself as I thought about how Sam and I had met. Oddly enough, we were both doing work-related errands, which brought us to the same grocery store. I had just finished the family's shopping list, and the baby was sleeping in a carrier on my back—or so I thought. I moved forward in the grocery line, and heard an "Ouch!" Somehow, the baby's hand had attached itself to Sam's hair and wouldn't let go.

"Oh my God, I'm so sorry!" I said.

Luckily, she was laughing. "It's okay. Totally my fault for making googly faces at your baby. I always do that, but usually I get away with it unnoticed." She was starting to shift her weight, embarrassed, because there were several pairs of eyes on us. I uncurled the tiny fingers from Sam's long, dark hair, and waited for her while she paid for her groceries, admiring how she seemed to do things with an "I dare you to mess with me" type attitude. She had a kind of rebelliousness that was hard to find in life and very refreshing. Her eyes were big and chocolate brown and she had dimples that would surely melt a guy.

"Actually, it's not my baby," I said, walking out with her. "I'm a nanny. Natalie. I would shake your hand, but mine are kinda full at the moment."

She smiled, looking at me, seeming to assess and understand everything about my life, all at once, like I had with her a few moments before. "Sam. Not short for anything, and it's not because my parents wanted a boy."

"Cool. Thanks for getting that out of the way early so I wouldn't have to bring it up later."

"Hey, no problem. I do my best to help a sista out."

I smiled, eyeing her bag. "Interesting groceries, if you don't mind my noticing."

She laughed. "I was wondering if you would. Actually, they're for my boss. I work at a bank and every Friday we hand out random prizes—for example, the first customer wearing a blazer, or a fedora, or the first person with an accent."

"Cool! Do the drive-through customers get prizes too?"

"Yep. They get a daily quiz. Completely random stuff."

"I wish my bank did that. I love the prizes!" The bag contained such randomness as bathtub floaty toys, one man ping pong, "Mad Libs", "See-A-Word" puzzles and an Etch-A-Sketch.

"Oooh, an Etch-A-Sketch!" I got excited, as I hadn't seen one of those since my childhood in Japan.

Without a second thought, she took it out of the bag and handed it to me. I smiled, speechless. "Well, you can come visit and set up a new account, if you like. I always get to do the shopping because I have the best sense of humor."

"Cool, I've actually been looking for a new bank anyway."

I walked along, grinning from ear to ear at the memory and how everything just seemed to flow from then on— with chaos sprinkled on top, as it were. We had gone to a concert two weeks later and realized we had tons in common. We'd both been really shy growing up, kind of outsiders. Neither one of us had the confidence to shine, then, or even cared to. And neither of us had ever been married or had kids, but had watched all our respective friends do both. Our age, by the way, was the same. I was a few months older.

I had backstage passes to said show, Maktub, a Seattle band, because I was connected like that. We met the band and they asked us, being cute groupies, to join them at the after-party. We of course said yes. Once we got there they said they were jamming with another band and asked if we would dance on stage with them. We, of course, said yes. And the rest was history. Literally. It would go down in the chronicles as the night those two chicks came from out of the blue, helped rock Seattle, and disappeared back into the dark of night. Little did they know, we had left the concert, and were on the ferry laughing about being on stage—until we met some drunken guys who we felt compelled to help find rides home. Everything that happened to us made us laugh harder and smile more. Ever since then, things just seemed to spark when we got together. It all seemed so...unplanned, though somehow orchestrated, by the Universe.

I laughed to myself at the memories of the past year, and kept walking around Chico, "population of roughly 100,000," which Sam had mentioned after I'd slept through our arrival. I was starting to get hot. Water would be good...*really* good. I turned around to go back to the apartment, when I realized I'd walked so far and made a few turns, and had absofreakinglutely no idea where I was.

Simple, I'll just call Sam and ask her how to get back. I opened my phone, realized I didn't have the bride-to-be's number and Sam's phone didn't work in Chico for some reason. Lame. Good one, Natalie. Such a together girl, but take her out of her surroundings and see what happens. Ha ha, very funny. Oh to be a crustacean right now. With my luck, I'd be one of the ones getting crunched.

It didn't feel funny though, it felt like...dehydration, hunger, thighs rubbing together in the heat, and panic setting in. I was officially disoriented. Now I knew how people lost in the desert felt. Well, sort of. I tried to do some deep breathing to calm myself, but it didn't work. Luckily, I saw a tree up ahead. Shade. I went to lean on it. I had my head back, hands on my eyes, thinking, I'm going to die out here and I turned down nookie last night. What's *wrong* with me? Even superheroes get lost sometimes. "I'm not going to cry," I recited. I felt the heat of tears. "Crap."

Then I heard a familiar sound: a fire engine.

I didn't believe it, but there it was, and it was getting louder and louder, until...it pulled onto the street I was on, and then there were three: Mickey and Marty, thousand-watt smiles blazing, shirtless, and an as-yet-unknown one, driving, and speaking on the loudspeaker. All of this was reverberating against the houses they drove by. Marty saw me first, hit Mickey on the arm, and Mickey yelled to the driver, "Wait, stop, I know her!"

The fire engine pulled to a stop, and thankfully, they turned the siren off, because that sucker was blowing my eardrums. Not to mention, this whole experience was blowing my mind. Mickey held a megaphone, into which he said, for the whole town to hear, "You thought you were finished with me, Natalie Newport, but no such luck!" I felt myself blushing. Luckily, I could use the heat as an excuse.

He got out, sauntered over, and asked me what I was doing. "Oh, just taking a walk," I said. I had to keep my cool. Even though I was in a new town, I *still* had a rep to protect.

"What are you guys doing?" I countered, smiling. I hadn't moved an inch from the tree I was leaning on. Just a few moments ago, I was panicked, and now I was standing here, famished but flirting. Call me crazy, but I was having trouble keeping up with the events of my own life. The little reporter in my head, Mini-Me, was speed talking. "Breaking news! Misplaced Washington nanny gets lost on the streets of Chico, California for hours and rescued by...you guessed it, firefighters. Yep. You heard it here first, ladies and gentlemen. Stay tuned to Channel NN for updates."

"See the banner and balloons? We are advertising our convention, to bring awareness to Chico and surroundings about the firefighter movement."

"Wow! So it's a movement, huh?"

"It is. Actually, we need more funding for more trucks and to hire more employees, because right now, if three fires happen at the same time in different areas of the county, the fire department is understaffed."

"I see. So you figure that raising hell, sirens blazing and shirts off will get people to throw money at you?"

"Pretty much."

"I see your point," I said, eyeing his chest and trying not to drool.

He laughed and grabbed my hand. "Come on," he said, pulling me toward the truck. He helped me climb in the front. I sat down, looked around and saw a gazillion gadgets. Mickey introduced me to the driver, Frank, an older, sweet looking guy. He opened his mouth, and out came remnants of Jersey. Frank quickly put his accent to use by getting back on the mic and shouting out the time and location of the picnic.

"We have a buffet-style picnic in the park today at two. We want people to come and enjoy themselves, so we're advertising," Mickey said over the shouting. He'd left Marty in the back to throw candy at the kids who'd come out to see the commotion. "We have to hit almost every street and we have just under two hours to do it. In a while, we're going to the mall."

"Wow, firefighters sure do things differently in California," I said, smiling on the outside at what I'd gotten myself into. Inside, I was thinking, "Sweet! Either we'll hit Abby's street or if not, I'll be able to look up the number in the phone book and call her so she won't think I was kidnapped." And that's exactly what I did.

I explained that I'd gotten lost, but didn't tell her about the fire truck. After she finished laughing at me, she asked if I was okay and gave me the address. After hanging up I went back to the fire truck and said, "Hey, there's a street I don't think you went down yet. It's where Sam is. Can we go there?"

"Sure thing, little lady," Frank said.

Meanwhile, Mini-Me continued the report: "Lost nanny not only found, folks, but she is going to pick up her friend so they can consort with firefighters all day long."

We pulled down the aforementioned street, sirens blazing, balloons flying, firemen waving. For this, they'd lent me a fire hat and put me in the back of the truck. We pulled up next to the apartment, Frank honked the horn twice, and Sam walked out, puzzled expression on her face, until she saw me. Smilingly, I followed her eyes as they scanned the banner, balloons, me, and finally to Frank, Mickey, and Marty. "Surprise!" I bellowed. She started to laugh.

"Come on, we're going to get some grub at the picnic!"

She flashed the "one sec" finger, and a moment later came out of the apartment ready to go. I was certain she had grabbed her purse and applied lipstick. Oh, and a spritz of perfume, as well. She climbed on back with me, gave me a huge bear hug, remarked on how she couldn't have imagined something this cool happening in a million years, because the bride-to-be was stressed, big time, so Sam needed a break. And we were off.

Sam and I left Chico two days later, still smiling. We had business to attend to. As it turns out, the bride-to-be chose not to come with us to the beach. She had her own business to attend to. There were no hard feelings. She just wasn't in the mental space to have a carefree good time. She was too busy making sure no one botched up her wedding, even though it was still months away.

The Redwoods were amazing. We drove through a hollow tree trunk, and I stood up and took a picture up the inside of the tree. We took all kinds of touristy photos, like both of us sitting on things carved out of the fallen trees, or both of us sitting and standing in different poses by the car.

Then we headed to the coast, with Sam as my tour guide. She'd been there many times, but somehow even with all my overseas travels, I had missed most of California. On our way out of the forest (which was the only way out), we found ourselves stopped behind about 50 cars, with no idea what was happening up ahead because it was too far away to see. When we saw the people in front of us (and in front of them), get out of their cars to put blankets on the ground to wait, we turned off the engine. Sam turned to me.

"So, you think we're here for the night?"

"Uhm."

"Yeah."

We cranked the tunes, but that lasted about 10 minutes before we got tired of it. I turned to Sam.

"So."

"So…"

"We're going to the beach next, right?"

"Yep."

"Half Moon Bay."

"Correct."

"Cool. Can't wait."

"Same here."

Wow. A few more minutes of such riveting conversation and we'd both fall asleep.

Which we did.

We awoke some time later to a very loud sound that we couldn't place, until we saw a tree falling up ahead at the start of the traffic backup. Then the sound of cheering broke out all around us. The people who had been lying on blankets were jumping up and down on the road. The guy picked up his girlfriend and swung her around in circles. The traffic started to move, so everyone scrambled into their cars and we inched along.

I was still resting my eyes when I heard Sam say, "Oh you have *got* to be kidding me."

I looked. I saw.

There were 20 firefighters standing on the side of the road. They cheered as we went past. Apparently, two hot chicks in a convertible were most welcome in the Golden State.

After we left the firefighters in our rear view mirror, I drifted off again. I had a dream that I was running through a forest. I didn't know where I was running. I didn't care, I was deliriously, deliciously running—away. Away from the reality of being home soon, of seeing Hammer, knowing I had no idea if he reciprocated my feelings, away from responsibility, away from knowing I'd soon have two toddlers to take care of, 10 hours a day. Away from always being responsible and acting my age. Running felt natural— whether it was toward something or away from it didn't much matter at this juncture.

When I awoke, I looked over at Sam. We smiled at each other, ready for the bliss of Half Moon Bay. I turned back to face forward just in time to see a *Crescent City Firefighters Welcome You* sign. "Oh, now I know you're joking, Universe."

"The sign?" Sam asked, smiling.

"Yeah. I really thought if I did something about it, the Universe would stop sending me signs and signals."

"Ah grasshoppa, it is the firefighter at *home* waiting that you must to do something about."

"I know, I know." I paused. "Does that mean Mickey was a freebie that I passed up?"

"Apparently."

"That's terrible news. I so miss martial arts, by the way. It really helps to kick the crap out of those pads."

"I can imagine."

"I miss my cat."

"Who's feeding your cat?"

"I have one of those feeders that releases enough food and water for a week."

"Ah."

"So my apartment might smell a little when I get home, but I use candles and Febreze to make it smell nice again."

"So?"

"You want to go back early?"

I thought about it. "Sure. We can see Half Moon Bay another time, right?" I asked, hoping we wouldn't live to regret this decision later.

"Definitely."

"I can borrow the Spyder to drive to my gym once, right?"

"You got it."

"Cool."

We found a hotel room—somewhat more easily, this time, and conked out for the night.

We stopped at a restaurant for breakfast on the way out of town. Walking in, a firefighter calendar greeted us. I picked one up. "You think the Universe is watching?"

"The Universe is always watching." Sam assured me.

"Do you think buying this will get me any brownie points?"

Sam smiled. "I'd say…if you didn't, I'm afraid of what might happen on the way home."

"Point taken," I said as we were shown to the table. I knew what I wanted to eat, so I started flipping through the calendar instead of the menu. When the waitress came, I said, "I'll have one of these," pointing to a tall drink of water known as February. She laughed, and said "Hey, I have one of those, and he is in this calendar!"

She flipped to August, and by God, there was Mickey, smiling out at us from the page—holding a hose, all suited up, except for a shirt. He even had the helmet and suspenders on. Oh my God, this waitress is Mickey's girlfriend! What are the chances? Oh my double God, I passed that up! And it had nothing to do with honor, either. Well, not that much to do with honor. Oh man oh man oh man. Calm down, do not let them see your inner panic, even though you surely have beads of sweat on your forehead. Breathe.

Sam had no idea that my innards were doing flip-flops at that moment, because she hadn't seen the photo, and was just laughing at how cosmically cool it was that everywhere we went, firefighters appeared. I smiled, and said "Not bad! I'd like to buy one. Would you put it in a bag for me?" As an afterthought, I added, "That Mr. February, phew!" I don't think I caused any suspicion.

When Sam and I finished eating, which I really couldn't do much of, we got back into the Spyder. It was my turn to drive, but I couldn't focus. My legs wobbled and stomach churned, so I just sat down in the driver's seat, facing toward the parking lot, and put my head between my knees.

Breathing deeply, I tried not to think of having spent the night in the same bed with the waitress's supposed boyfriend. Even though nothing happened, I felt terrible. Ninja Nanny had a conscience—who knew?

Sam thought I had heat stroke, not being used to the California sun. I let her think so, because I couldn't speak. She got me some water and threatened to find a firefighter to hose me down. I still had my head down, but started to laugh so she knew I was okay.

For once, there were no firefighters around to help us. I managed to move into the passenger seat, and Sam drove all the way to a little town called Trinidad, which had been recommended to us by the waitress.

We stood at an overlook, staring out at the vast Pacific. This was the widest view of the ocean I'd ever seen. The sun poked through the clouds and the little rock islands below were encircled by mist.

"Beautiful, ain't it Thelma?"

"Sure is, Louise."

We sighed in unison.

"This ain't the end of our journey, is it Thelma?" Sam asked.

"No it ain't, Louise," I replied, smiling wistfully. "It ain't easy like in the movies. That's why there are movies—we need an escape from the intricate weave of reality."

"Yeah, I know." We were on the same page with our thoughts, plugging them into our own realities. We just kept looking at the mist and water for another long moment.

For five minutes, we had been speaking with Southern accents. Some elderly people sitting on a bench nearby probably didn't realize that we weren't actually from the South. This is why I loved road trips. You could be whoever you wanted and no one would know if you were faking. Occasional, liberating insanity for sanity's sake.

After the break, I was feeling better and ready to drive. Nothing like sea air to awaken the senses. I wasn't ready to tell Sam just yet what had happened at the restaurant. I just wanted to make sure the queasiness didn't come back.

We stopped to get gas, and I swear the dog in the pickup next to us smiled at me. I was beginning to wonder if the Universe ever stopped laughing at us.

Back on the road, I remarked, "I can't believe I went to California without actually touching water and sand." Sam just smiled.

I drove and drove along the winding coast. Then, guess what. We found the coolest beach ever. We just turned a corner, and there it was; this big, sprawling beach calling our names. I looked over at her. "Did you know this was here?"

"Nope." There was that twinkle again. Sam had some secrets of her own.

We hit the Evergreen State in the late afternoon, keeping the top down and blasting the heat. "Back to life, back to reality," I sang. Sam joined in. We were trying to keep the mood light, but I know we both wanted more vacation. I smiled at the memories, thanked Sam for fueling and funding the adventure, and put the car in park in front of her apartment.

We had officially exhausted the Road Trip CDs. The presets on the stereo were all Seattle stations. That part I'll admit was nice, to hear voices of familiar DJ's as we rolled into town. Then, we heard John Mayer's voice singing, "My dear, we're slow dancing in a burning room." I grinned and looked at Sam to see if she was tuned in, which of course she was—her eyes met mine and I saw the humor in them. I changed the station.

"Cause when we kiss…oooh, fire." The Pointer Sisters. We looked at each other. I switched it to another station.

"I was so high I did not recognize the fire burning in your eyes…" Maroon 5. I switched it again.

"Come on baby light my fire." The Doors. Again, I changed it.

"Love…is a burning thing. And it makes…a fiery ring." Johnny Cash. Sam looked at me. I pressed the next button.

"Burn baby burn, disco inferno." Sam laughed, and I changed it again.

"World on fire, more than I can handle." Sarah McLachlan. And another switch.

"We didn't start the fire…it was always burning since the world's been turning." Billy Joel.

I looked at Sam. "*You* do it." She did it.

"You're fired!" It was an ad for The Apprentice. Even The Donald was getting in on this cosmic joke.

"To me, it merely speaks. To you, it sings," she said in her best narrator voice. I just shook my head, looking down. Sam laughed and got out. She laughed all the way to her doorstep, turned, and said "It's been a pleasure being pawns in the Universe's game with you. Now go forth and do what you know you must." She saluted, and I saluted her back.

"Yes, captain."

I took a deep breath and drove the convertible straight to the gym. It was a gorgeous, sunny summer day and I was oblivious to the stares I was getting. I was laser focused on my objective: Hammer.

Finally, I was driving a car that sizzled. I parked, licked the tip of my finger, put it on my derriere, and made the "sss" sound. In my best movie narrator voice, I said, "Ninja Nanny—nobody's bitch." I had to get into the right frame of mind to see Hammer. This was mood-setting behavior at its finest. The attitude attire was already in place. I had on a leather tank top, leather pants, boots that zipped up to the knee, sunglasses, and the beginnings of a killer tan. Today, I would sport the leather—before working out, of course—to catch his eye. I paused outside the door, scanned the parking lot for the fire trucks, and saw that they were there. And it was good.

Normally, I didn't have to inflate myself like this. Not for martial arts, where it's best to remain humble or be defeated by the ego before the sparring starts. But for firefighter-related matters, I definitely needed the boost.

Making a Splash

"Please, please, please let him be here," I recited to myself. He only worked out every other day, and his schedule changed constantly so I wasn't sure. Sam didn't have to return the Spyder until 10pm, but I was still on the clock.

I checked in and looked around. The receptionist told me the owner (my martial arts teacher) was in the café if I was looking for him. I said thanks, walked around the corner, and saw his shiny brown ponytail. He didn't show surprise often, but this time I got a whistle and an eyebrow raise.

"I see California was good to you!" I detected a twinkle in those chocolate brown eyes.

"Very," I smiled warmly and hugged his shoulder.

"Are you here to work out today?"

"Yep. I'm just going to do some light cardio and weights." This was my way of letting him know there was no need to meet me downstairs to train. "I'm starting a new nanny job tomorrow, so I have some prep work to do for that."

"Great. Good luck to you."

We flashed our secret sign—anyone watching might've thought it was a gang sign, but it really meant "Balance. Beyond the limits." Someday, I'd have to learn more about my teacher. He was pretty mysterious though, so I didn't ask questions. I figured when the time was right, he'd invite me into his world.

I walked into the cardio area. There was Hammer, on the elliptical. It was as if no time had passed. He noticed me, gave me the once over, and smiled. His co-workers noticed too. I gave a small smile and nod, and kept walking. I ducked into the bathroom and quick-changed into my workout clothes.

I was thinking how just seeing him was cardio in itself as it raised my heart rate, as I went to do a couple stretches to get rid of the car stiffness, and give them time to get off the elliptical so I could use it.

As I stretched, I thought about how nice the new parents of the kids I'd be watching were. During the interview, they agreed to let me bring the kids to the gym for Kids' Club three times a week, so that I could work out in the mornings and have energy for the rest of the day. I knew this would really help. So I'd do cardio and weights in the mornings and then martial arts at night.

I used martial arts in combination with what I had learned about resistance training, and with yoga. I did child's pose for relaxation, then moved into downward dog—I loved this pose, because with the body in an upside down V, your back, arms and legs get stretched at the same time. Then in cobra pose, I propped my torso up with my arms in the appropriate snake-like fashion. I thought about the trip. A significant amount of energy, or chi, had been released on this trip, because Sam and I had reverted back to our younger days. It was wonderful. Yet now I needed to re-harness my energy. I did the warrior poses and felt better.

I moved to the elliptical, and then the treadmill. This one had moving feet and arm handles which was much better for me than doing the flat treadmill. To each her own, but the more I could move at once, the more calories were burned and stress released.

Sometimes, I couldn't help tuning in to what was on TV. I didn't make a habit of doing this, it just happened once in a while, especially if something caught my eye. I had been chided by my trainer for doing it—zoning out, he called it. He taught us to always focus our minds on the task at hand, to be in the moment. But I called it multi-tasking; when I watched TV, it made me stay on the machine longer and therefore burn more calories. I still alternated between going as fast as I could at low resistance and then at a high resistance; I just did more intervals because there was a good show on.

Today, a rerun of Ellen caught my eye. She had John Travolta on, which was great. I liked him. They were talking about Ladder 49, and of course, after a commercial break, they put on the full firefighter garb. And then, they started taking it all off, to music. It was a firefighter striptease. They were both laughing really hard, and so was I. Oh, the irony.

I flipped open my phone, and dialed Sam. "You'll never guess what's on."

"What?"

I told her all about the show. "I thought these signs were supposed to stop after the trip was over."

"No, grasshoppa. They will only stop when you do something about the firefighter you love. You must solve the mystery. Is he there?"

"Yes."

"Then go. Now." And she hung up.

Well, that was a fine how do you do. I expected a least a little sympathy, or at the very least, some specific advice—which I guess she gave me. I decided to take it.

I walked in to the weight room, where they were all working out near each other. Didn't they ever split up? How deep did this brotherhood go, anyway, jeeze?

"Can I speak to you for a moment?"

He didn't hesitate. "Sure." We walked a few feet away. With the music playing, we were outside of hearing distance from his buddies.

"I want to show you something. How long of a break do you have to work out?"

"Actually, I did the early shift. I'm off," he said.

Score! "Meet me outside in 20 minutes?"

"Done."

That was cool, considering I barely knew him. Oh, we'd had several conversations while side-by-side on the treadmill, but nothing that had pushed us over the line to socializing outside the club.

I knew enough about him though, to know he was of good character, and single. I knew he played guitar, listened to Dave Matthews, and loved watching Jet Li movies, so we were good there. I also knew he got excited about watching sports, which was wonderful to me. You see, I needed my "me time," big time, and if a guy wanted to be with me 24/7/365, that was, for lack of a better word, icky. I don't know whether it was from being alone for so many years or what, but I just couldn't live like that, attached at the hip all the time.

The rest of the information I had was from reading him at the gym. I knew he was naturally cool, but underneath, he was a big teddy bear. I could see tickling the heck out of him, and that he'd love it. I knew he used to be somewhat of wild child, but had mellowed out a bit. I knew he needed to be gradually, gracefully reminded that life wasn't over, and that age was just a number.

I gradually, gracefully drove the silver bullet up to the entrance to the gym, just as he was walking out. Perfect. I pressed the "Top down, baby, oh yeah" button. What can I say? The car had the voice of Barry White. It was just that smooth.

He stood there, checking out the ride. "Whoa." He had a smile like Josh Holloway from Lost—sweet enough to give you cavities, with that little dimple on the left. And eyes like Joaquin Phoenix. If it was possible to swoon in a car, that's exactly what I was doing. Good thing I had shades on. He got in. "Is it yours?"

"Just until 10pm tonight. A friend and I went to California for the weekend. We wanted to ride in style."

"I see. Is this what you wanted to show me?"

"It's part of it."

All of a sudden, I heard a huge honking sound, over and over, and saw some flashing lights and a whoop whooping sound. And then there was the siren. His firefighter buddies were sitting in the engine, giving him some love—some really loud love.

"Oh, wow," I said, laughing and shaking my head.

"If we hurry, I think we can escape."

"I'm on it." I revved the engine and whipped around the corner out of sight. They tried, but the huge beast couldn't keep up.

I hit the freeway, and a minute later, nudged his arm and said, "Psst, I think we lost 'em."

He flashed me that wide grin, and asked where we were going.

"That's for me to know and you to find out, mister."

"Yes ma'am."

I utilized the exit of choice, and gracefully executed the turns until I found the road I was looking for—a long straight stretch. I got up to 90mph, turned to Hammer and said, "Are we having fun yet?"

"Yep." He smiled but looked nervous. He was either getting a little scared or wanting to drive, so instead of speeding up, I slowed down. I understood his fear, if it was that. A deer might've run out into the road at any second and that would not be pretty. His desire to drive, I could also understand, but his name wasn't on the contract and I didn't want to get Sam into trouble.

I turned off onto a long road that turned into a one-lane dirt road after a bit. We came to a stop at the rippling edge of a beautiful, glassy lake.

"Whoa!" he said. "I never knew this was here." I just smiled. We got out, walked to the edge, and leaned on the Spyder's hood.

"I thought you'd like it."

"How'd you know it was here?"

"Hiking trip. Girl Scouts, circa 2002."

He chuckled. "I was a Boy Scout."

"Hate it?"

"Yep. You?"

"Uh huh."

I glanced at him. His eyes seemed to focus and see straight through to my soul. I didn't know how he did that. I grabbed his hand. "Come on."

We walked hand in hand for a few minutes, my pulse racing. I wondered if he could feel it. We arrived at an abandoned hut, with an abandoned canoe in it. "Help me with this," I said.

"What? It might leak!"

"Only one way to find out!"

We put it in the water and I gingerly climbed aboard. There was a paddle covered with moss and spider webs. He grabbed it, cleaned it off and pushed the canoe out from the shore with it.

We drifted in silence for a few minutes, facing each other, and he said he thought we were safe.

"Thanks for coming out here with me," I said.

"Sure. I'm always up for an adventure," he replied. I was hoping he'd throw me a bone and let me know he'd had his eye on me too, but it didn't seem like he wanted to share that info.

"My friends and I talk about you sometimes," he said. Maybe I was wrong.

"Really? And what do you say?"

"Mostly, wondering what you're about, who you are. What goes through that head of yours while you're working out...that kind of thing."

"I see..."

"Well, plus the obvious."

"What's the obvious?"

"How hot you are."

At that point, my stomach dropped out of my body, into the bottom of the boat and into the lake. Or so it felt. I'm sure my face turned all kinds of red, too, so I looked up at the sky and said, "What a beautiful day, don't you think?"

He laughed. "Yes, it's gorgeous." But I knew he wasn't talking about the day. I felt his energy surrounding me, and there was that heat—the heat I craved. There was a low hum in my stomach. Other than that, all I knew at that moment was that I felt totally comfortable with him, and totally excited—at the same time. I didn't know how this was possible, but the fusion of the two was hypnotic.

I was happy now that Mickey and I hadn't done anything on the trip. It was sweet and good fun, but it just didn't feel…right. This flashed through my mind for a beat, and I smiled to be in the moment I was in right now, with Hammer.

"Natalie…" he moved towards me. He didn't do it gracefully though. Somehow he lost his balance and then tried to regain it, but the canoe tipped over.

I came out of the water, instantly thankful that I'd worn waterproof mascara today, and a bit panicked about the cell phone he had on him. "Did your—"

"I left it in the car," he said, cutting me off.

"Oh. I was really scared you might've…wait. Isn't that against the rules?"

"Not when I'm off duty. Actually, not when I'm busy."

"So that's how it is."

"Yeah. I guess I didn't want to be bothered."

"Wait. Did you really do the early shift this morning?"

"Nope." This time the smile that grew across his face was mischievous.

I shook my head, smiling too. "You mean you got off early just to hang out with me?"

"When the boss heard you wanted to show me something, he was all for it. He's a softy that way. I knew he'd let me off."

"That's pretty confident of you, sir."

"I'm a confident guy."

We heard a gurgle, and looked over as the last of the canoe submerged.

"Looks like we're swimming," he observed.

"Good way to warm up."

"I know a better one." And he grabbed my waist and pulled me in close. He put his big hand on my hair and face, and kissed me. He had strong lips. His hands moved down to the small of my back, and the warmth that ran through me to the core is indescribable. I don't know how long we kissed there in the water, but it was the best first kiss I've ever had.

Finally, he opened his eyes, looked at me deeply for a long moment and smiled. He turned around, put my arms over his shoulders so I was on his back, and swam us in.

I still had a towel in the car from the road trip, which we used to dry off as much as possible, and I drove him back to the club. My hand rested on the gear shift and he put his over mine. I shivered as I thought about how he knew exactly what to do in the moment and wasn't afraid to do it. He put his jacket over me. We pulled up and he thanked me for making his day completely unlike what he thought it'd be when he woke up that morning.

"You're most welcome," I said, not sure if the purring sound was from the engine or from me. He leaned over and kissed me goodbye, for a good 2-3 minutes.

I started my new job with a positive attitude—fresh from vacation and from kissing a hot guy in the water. I was recharged and ready to whip these kids into shape.

All I had to do on this first day was wake them up, get them dressed, take the oldest to school, make sure they had plenty of healthy snacks, change diapers, and work on their manners, as instructed by Camalia and Carl. Then I had to pick the boy up from school and entertain them for the next few hours (minus naptime, of course) until the C's (that's what I called the parents) got home. It was all doable. It was all cake for Ninja Nanny.

Right up until I had to wake them up, that is. I decided to start with Cameron. When I met the family, I observed his excess energy, and a definite inferiority complex because of his cute little sis, who was only a little over a year younger than his 3.5 years. His little body held a commanding stature. He was like a tiny adult and his body language said he knew where he was going and how to get there. So I figured getting him up and about first today would make him feel special, and then I could enlist his aid in picking out his sister's clothing. I imagined him a great little helper. Unfortunately, my imagination wasn't always spot on.

Being consistent is key, I thought to myself. This was to be my mantra in the coming months.

I crept into his room and just looked for a moment. He looked so peaceful, brown curls and sweet long chestnut eyelashes. I nudged his arm. He stirred, stretched, and opened his hazel eyes halfway. Then his lip curled and he said, "No," with an attitude and turned over onto his left side, his back to me.

"So it's like that, is it? We'll see."

I tickled him. He giggled and screamed with delight. So much for getting him dressed before his sister woke up. She was in a crib, so she couldn't get out until I took her out.

"Ready to get up, little man?"

"No."

I picked him up and said, "Now, pick out your clothes."

"No."

"Okay, I'll help you."

"No! I do myself." Such defiance flashed in those little eyes.

"Fine."

He walked over to his dresser, opened a drawer, and rummaged through the whole thing, throwing clothes all over his room. Was this what his parents allowed or was this just a test for his new nanny?

"No, that's not how you choose your clothes. You do it like this," I said, showing him how to go through the drawer calmly. Instead of listening to me, he started running all over his room, jumping on the clothes he'd just thrown around. "Ayayayayayeeeeee!" I started picking them up and putting them in the dresser, ignoring his behavior, not wanting to reinforce it. He was trying to get a reaction out of me, but I wouldn't give. *Keep your cool, Natalie. Lose control, and you've lost him.*

Eventually, I'd ignored his antics for long enough that he stopped and joined me at the dresser. "Which one would you like to wear to school today?" I asked, holding out two shirts. *Limit the options to 2.*

"No." And with that, he ran into his sister's room and started yelling her name. "Courtney! Courtneyyy good morning, good morning, good good good morningningningning!"

I could see this was going to take more work than I thought. I walked into Courtney's bedroom, where she was still lying on her back, hiding behind her stuffed animals. "Good morning, Courtney! Cameron and I will be right back," I said, taking him by the hand. He started pulling away from me.

"No, I don't want to go school! Noooo!" and he fought with all the strength his 3.5 years could muster, which was actually quite a bit. But I was stronger.

I picked him up and carried him into his room, while he was wriggling, crying and screaming in my ear. I put him down in front of the dresser. "Don't waste your energy fighting with me, Cameron," I said calmly. "Let's pick out your clothes so we can go have some yummy breakfast." I gave him the widest smile I could muster in the moment.

He was still crying, but he agreed, grudgingly. "Okay," he said, sniffing and wiping his eyes.

"Now, do you want the Spiderman shirt or the Bob the Builder shirt?"

"Spiderman!"

"Okay! How about jeans?"

We managed to pick out underwear, socks and jeans with a normal amount of toddler fuss, and then it was time for Courtney.

I walked into her room. "Well, hello Courtney!" I said brightly. She just looked at me, as if to say, who are you and why are you in my room? I tried to grab her, but she protested. Instead, she wanted to show me her stuffed animals—all five of them, one by one. So I met each one, and then she let me pick her up. The feeling of her head resting on my shoulder was really sweet. Cameron was dancing around my feet the whole time, trying to get my attention.

I put Courtney on the changing table, grabbed a diaper, and started taking off her pajamas. She did her very best to hold her arms down so that I couldn't take off her pajama shirt. When I finally got it off, she tried to keep me from taking off the shorts. I ignored this and went about my job. She finally realized she wasn't getting anywhere by resisting, so she quit. It had taken me a full 20 minutes since I'd gotten into her room to get her undressed to get the diaper on. Now we were on to picking out her outfit. She had about 8,000 of them to choose from, or so it seemed.

"Okay, Court, which shirt do you want?" I held up two. She pointed at one of them, so I put the other one in the drawer.

"No, not dat one! Da udder one!!!" she screamed.

"Okay. Cameron, can you get the other one please?"

"Sure!" He went to the dresser and picked it out.

"No, not dat one, da udder one!" she said with delight.

"Okay, Courtney," I said, holding them both up. "Which one do you want, or you can go naked and freeze outside in the cold." She thought about this for a second, taking it as a joke at first.

When she laughed and I didn't, she said "Mmm, dat one!" she said. She tried to fight me while I put it on, saying she wanted the other one and screaming as I pulled it over her head, but I succeeded in dressing her by having Cameron help me pick the rest of the outfit.

"Your brother is going to choose your jeans and socks today!" I said, trying to make it fun. She did the same thing with him, rejecting his choices, but we finally got the little princess dressed.

They ran around me while we went downstairs, and then I sat them at the little booth where they ate. They both had their own seats, and fought me on going into them, squirming and kicking and saying what I now realized was their favorite word: "No."

Choose your battles. Make each punishment related to each crime, as much as possible. Once they knew they wouldn't get anywhere with their behavior, they would stop the behavior. Right?

They were fascinated watching me make the small portions of hashed browns and bacon. It was one of the things their mom made them regularly. I looked in the pantry, and saw a bunch of cereals: sugar, sugar and more sugar. No wonder these kids acted like they were on speed. Mental note: gradually replace this junk with healthy yet tasty cereals like flavored oatmeal, etc. They don't need 10 different unhealthy options, just a few good ones. Add fruit. Make scrambled eggs with tiny avocado chunks. Just because the C's let the kids take over in the kitchen doesn't mean I have to. I didn't put this here, so it might be harder to take away, but not impossible. I hope.

We got their shoes on with a bunch of going back and forth from the front to the back door to get shoes and jackets. Cameron could put his on but could not tie them himself yet. Courtney needed help with the whole process. It was not easy putting her shoes on with Cameron, who had climbed onto my back, sitting and bucking on my shoulders like he was riding a bronco at the rodeo, but I did it. I calmly removed him, took a deep breath and walked out the door to tackle the car seats.

There were a bunch of things for toddlers to hurt themselves on in the garage, so I had to watch with an eagle eye. I opened a door to the SUV and Cameron climbed in. He kept leaning down to try and buckle the belt himself and I couldn't see what I was doing. "Cameron, let Natalie do it." Then he thought it was a game.

"No." He smiled.

"You're going to get tickled if you don't let Natalie do it."

"No."

"Okay..." I tickled him until I was sure he was just about to pee his pants, and then he stopped. I clicked the belt into place, closed the door and went over to Courtney's side. She was in the middle of the backseat, standing up, and had already taken her shoes and socks off. Oy vey.

"Courtney, get in your seat please."

"No."

"I'm going to count to three. If Courtney is not in her seat by three, I will tell mommy and daddy she was a bad girl today. One." She thought about it for a second. "Two." Apparently the thought of possibly being punished later was enough motivation for her. She moved into her seat with speed and agility. "Three. Very good, Courtney." Her car seat was a little harder for Natalie to figure out. I felt like I was wearing a big fat "duh" sign on my forehead. Luckily though, no neighbors were watching. I figured it out and went to the front of the car.

"See? I am getting in and putting my seat belt on right away. Natalie gets an A+."

"Natalie, Natalie, can we get an A+ too?"

"If you get right into your seats and wait quietly for Natalie to buckle you in, you will get an A+." I could hear their little brains thinking about this. I knew I'd have to bribe them.

Sure enough, the next words out of Cameron's mouth were, "Can we have candy if we get an A+?" The C's had told me no candy, but I figured no harm in kids getting candy in moderation. There were some things that parents didn't need to know. If these tactics worked, I was sure as swizzle sticks not going to eliminate them. I was strict, but not stupid.

"Yes, maybe you can have candy if you get an A+. We'll see. What's your favorite kind of candy?"

"M n M's," they both said at once.

"What else do you like?"

Cameron thought about it. "Reese's Pieces. Butterfinger."

Every time he would say something, Courtney would say "Mmm!"

"Oreo's."

"Mmm! Yummm!"

"Ice cream!"

"Mmm! Yummm!" Every time, her exclamation would get a little louder. She was right behind me, so it was giving me the slightest, tiniest infinitesimal smidge of the beginnings of a headache.

We dropped Cameron off at school, and I noticed they had a mini basketball court and a little running track—how perfect for burning excess energy.

Courtney and I went to the park. She loved to swing. My arms were pretty tired after two hours of swinging, but as much as they hurt, I needed the brain break from candy and kids. Before I knew it, it was time to pick Cameron up. Courtney screamed and cried when I took her out of the swing. Passers by would surely think I was committing bloody murder. I spoke softly to her. "We're going to pick up your brother now and have some lunch. Are you ready to eat?"

"Hmm…yes." And we had liftoff. At least the sun was shining and it was warming up. By the time I got her into her seat, grabbed Cameron and his backpack and buckled him in, I already needed a coffee so I took off for the nearest coffee stand, telling the kids we were taking a detour. I knew they didn't have a Blue's Clue what a detour was, but I wanted them to think it was something fun so I opened all the car windows. The wind blew through their hair and they looked at each other with smiles of surprise and delight. These kids were going to feel pressured to be overachievers, and I wanted to inject a little fun whenever I could.

Cameron said, "Courtie! Is your window open too?"

"Yes!" Courtney said.

"Woohoo!" I said.

"Woohoo!" they copied. I was sure I'd pay for teaching them "woohoo" later, but I didn't care. I knew Camalia and Carl had never done this, from the kids' reaction. The C's were occupied with parent stuff that I didn't have to worry about right now. Well, it's all relative, and I was relatively worry free. So I could go "woohoo."

The barista was male, in his mid 40's. He gave me a knowing look as we pulled up. "What'll it be, ma'am?"

"One grandé peppermint mocha please, sir."

"What's mocha, what's mocha?" Cameron asked.

"Nanny candy." I said. He didn't know what to do with that, so he was quiet. Until the barista broke out the cup of lollipops, that is. They weren't the cheap kind, either, but the kind that would last a while to lick.

"This okay?" he asked me.

"Sure." And I mouthed the words, "Bless you."

"What color do you want, kids?" I asked.

"Yellow!"

"Red!"

"Green!"

"Purple!"

"Blue!"

"Orange!"

"They don't want the moon, but they do want the rainbow," I said, laughing and hoping he didn't think these were my kids. I unwrapped them, handed them back, and enjoyed the blissful silence the suckers would give me. The lollipops, of course, not the kids.

"Are they yours?"

"Nope."

"I didn't think so. It would be a stretch to say they looked like you. So you're the nanny," he said with a grin.

"Natalie."

"Nice to meet you, Natalie. I'm Elliot." He paused. "Have you seen that nanny show?"

"Yep, I've seen it, and I've gotten a lot of tips from her. She rocks." But at least she is able leave after a short time and then the family is on its own, I thought to myself. These are my charges now, spoiled as they may be, and I'm responsible for what happens to them when mom and dad are at work. Sigh.

"She is great," he agreed. "I raised five girls, so I know a little something about it."

"Oh my. What a...mixed blessing," I said.

"Indeed." The cars were lining up behind me, so I said my goodbyes. "Come back soon!" he called. It was so easy with the kids strapped into their seats that I was starting to think driving 24/7/365 was an excellent plan. Until the need to poo and pee impeded it, of course.

I parked for a minute, telling the kids I needed air, flipped open my phone, got out of my car and leaned on the door. First, I dialed my trainer and got his voicemail. "This is Phoenix. I'm going to need some new challenges this week. This job is harder than I thought and I need balance." Then, I dialed Sam and got her voicemail. "I need girl time, stat. Hang tonight? Let me know." Who else did I want to call? Oh. This one made me smile.

Stop. Hammertime. The other calls were about what I needed. This one was about what he needed. Namely, Natalie.

Checking to see if the kids were okay with their lollipops and making faces at them through the window to entertain, I left a message on his voicemail, "You, me, wine, candle lit dinner. My place, 7pm tomorrow night. Sound good?"

The kids were still in rare form. They wouldn't settle down in the back seat, so I told them whoever was the quietest, the longest, would get an A+ and a fruit salad with whipped cream when we got home. They loved whipped cream and it was a great way to get them to eat fruit. They didn't have to know that I would use the sugar free stuff.

This trick worked for 8.5 minutes. I timed it. I thought it might be some sort of toddler world record. Courtney was the winner; I knew Cameron would steal some of her salad, which was all part of my devious plan not to have to force feed fruit.

I took the long way home, a winding road that followed the water, which took about a half hour to reach to the end, and came out right near their house.

They had a DVD player in the back of the car. With high hopes, I popped in Baby Einstein and pressed play. I thought this would work wonders to distract them, but not today. They were both singing a song Cameron had learned at school— at the top of their lungs, and I felt the wrinkle between my eyebrows deepening with each decibel.

By the time the trip was over, I had made several stops, trying Baby Bach, Baby Beethoven, Baby Galileo, Baby Da Vinci, and Baby Mozart. By the time I got to Baby MacDonald - a Day on the Farm, they were finally out cold. The thing about a sugar high is that it's most often followed by a sugar low. This knowledge of the workings of the Universe was very powerful and pleased me immensely.

I checked my messages. Sam had called back and confirmed that we were on for tonight.

After the C's dismissed me for the day, I sped home and made for the shower, letting go of the day, watching it disappear down the drain. It wasn't enough. I started the bath water running. I lounged in the water for the longest time, thinking of absolutely nothing. Then I wrapped myself in a big purple towel and fell into bed.

I woke up when the doorbell rang. It took me a minute, but I made it to the door and nobody was there. Instead, a bunch of stargazer lilies sat there with a tiny envelope attached. I looked around, picked them up and shut the door.

"To Natalie. Hoping the kids aren't making you insane yet." It wasn't signed. I wasn't familiar with the handwriting, but they had to be from Hammer. Right? He sure knew how to charm a woman's heart. At the perfect moment, too. He knew my favorite flower, too, but how?

I hurried and threw some makeup on, took one last whiff of the gorgeous flowers, grabbed my purse and left to meet Sam at our usual hangout. It was a cheesy, over-decorated Asian place. One side was a restaurant, and one a bar, with a dance floor in the middle. The place absolutely lacked ambiance, and that became its own sort of ambiance. There was usually a bored DJ spinning for the empty dance floor. Well, empty until we got there. We loved dancing and from there, observing the drunk people with amusement.

Sam was already seated, and had an appetizer sampler waiting. This was our favorite.

"Love you for this."

"I know," she said through a smirk.

She asked me how I was doing. I gave her the brief overview, and she commiserated. I told her about the flowers, and she smiled. Then her smile changed. She had the definite Mona Lisa mystery going on now.

"What's up?" I asked, giving her a look.

"Marty is flying up to see me."

"Oh my God!"

"That's what I said."

"I didn't even know you two had exchanged numbers!"

"Sorry, I forgot to mention that," she said.

"When?"

"This coming weekend."

"Sweet!"

"I know. I'm just thrilled."

"Wow! That's wonderful! Thanks, because I really needed some good news tonight. I'm so happy you get to see Marty again."

"Believe me, so am I." I had never seen Sam so ecstatic, in all our years of friendship.

"Let's toast this!" I said, raising my Coke Zero.

As we put our sodas down, suddenly I thought of the calendar and the waitress. Now, having seen these memories processing across my face, Sam was the one asking me what was up. "I have a confession to make."

"Really? Do tell," she said, intrigued.

I raised my glass and said with a perfectly straight face, "From the Redwood Forest, to the Gulf Stream waters, this land was made for you and me."

She laughed. "I'm listening."

I explained about the calendar and the waitress and me putting things together in the restaurant, and feeling sick because of it. Her eyes got really wide at the story. "I know. Not-so-much happenstance or coincidence, right?!"

"For sure. I'm trippin' now. What an intricate web we weave. Or that the cosmos does."

"Undeniably."

We both sat there for a minute. I let it sink in to her brain while she processed. "Sorry, didn't mean to lay all this on you at once, but I had to fess up. Just didn't have much time to recap when we got home."

"It's okay. You told me about the most important thing—the little swim you took with Hammer."

I smiled really wide. I couldn't help it. I wondered if he had called, so I pulled my cell out of my purse and checked messages. Sure enough, there was one from him, accepting for tomorrow night. As much as I wanted to stay there with Sam and party on, I had prep to do for the kids for the next day, and I needed to figure out what I'd make Hammer for dinner.

As I walked her to her car, a fire engine came out of nowhere, and almost hit me while turning the corner. I looked at Sam. "Well that was a nice near miss. Can you believe this?"

"Either way, the firefighters will screw ya," she said.

I laughed and high five'd her goodnight. Then I remembered what I wanted to give her. "Wait."

"Wha...?"

"Here. Now you can say you're dating Mr. October." Marty smiled out at her. I left her in shock, standing there, holding the page of the calendar I had torn out. "Nighty night," I said, hugging her shoulder and getting into my car.

When I got home, Kiki greeted me warmly, giving purrs and figure eights, hugging my ankles. Humans could learn so much from animals... how to greet the ones you love, for instance. You should always give a hug or kiss, or purr. ☺

I glanced at the flowers on the table and wondered if they were really from Hammer, or if they were actually from Mickey. They both knew about my new job. I wouldn't mention them to Hammer tomorrow night, and see if he: a) smiled knowingly, or b) looked quizzically when he saw them. Either way it'd be fine. I was very honest when it came to talking about the past, whether recent or ancient.

"Courtney, please get in your seat," I said firmly, the next morning.

"No."

"You do it, or I do it."

"No, *I*," she said in her most defiant tone, which was pretty darn defiant.

"All right." She got in the seat, and then she wanted to do the buckle, so I let her try.

"Can't do it," she said, sighing and throwing up her hands in a gesture of defeat. She was pursing her lips and it was so cute. All of this cute gesturing was just in the nick of time, before the vein in my forehead popped from waiting for her for the trillionth time that day.

Carl and Camalia had advised that I adopt routines with the kids early on. Therefore, I was trying to establish a routine for getting her in her seat. I had to let her try, or else she'd start crying. The trying took up at least three extra minutes, which was about ten less than the crying. Yesterday, it made us a few minutes late to Cameron's preschool. Today, I tried waking them up a few minutes earlier, but this just made them cranky. So I took all the dilly dallying they did in stride. If I worried too much about being exactly on time, I was going to give myself an ulcer.

My mission was to tackle their table manners, which were atrocious, and to get them to settle down come naptime. It was like constantly fighting Crouching Tiger *and* Hidden Dragon. I didn't have a choice which one, just which one to deal with first.

At least the C's were willing to work with me regarding preschool. They were thinking of adding another day per week, which would really work for me. Currently, Cameron was only there for three hours, three days a week, and his energy level was so high that the mornings without him were a blessing.

Today was not such a day, however. We were all going to my gym, where I took the kids to Kids' Club. I was allowed to work out for two hours a day, two days a week. I encouraged them to make new friends, but they were both shy in new situations. I figured the friendships would come from initial arguments and the sitters would teach them to make amends. I was wrong. The babysitters said they were wonderful and quiet. I slapped my forehead. "Huh? You're not inventing that, are you?"

"Nope. They just quietly watched TV and played with toys."

Okay, either they were doing my trick of telling the parents the kids were perfect that day to not make waves, or the kids were truly on good behavior and must be saving all the bad behavior for me. I suspected it was the latter. Not good.

After my workout, I was rejuvenated and refreshed. I couldn't wait to make them lunch and put them to bed so I could just have some time to think.

I cut up some apple slices and gave those to the kids for an appetizer, and made taquitos for their main course.

Cameron looked up at me with an earnest expression on his face like he was about to ask me something of dire importance. "Natalie, are taquitos made from mosquitoes?"

I lost it, almost spitting out my own lunch. "Yes, Cam, they are."

"Oh," he said, and went on eating. "Courtie, we're eating mosquitoes!"

"Alright!" she said.

"Woohoo!"

"Woohoo!"

Sometimes these two were just too much. Funny thing was, one minute they had adorable, angelic faces looking up at me, and the next, they were evoking the INXS song, Devil Inside, to play inside my head. They started horsing around at the table, so I said they could have 15 minutes outside. They played in the sandbox while I watched, and Cameron started dumping shovels full of sand on his sister. At first, she was delighted and then she started screaming and crying, and telling him to stop. I went to intervene, and Cameron hurled a bucketful of sand right at my face, which he'd obviously had ready for me. I grabbed his hand.

"Inside. *Now.*"

He yanked away from me. "NO!" He started running around the backyard laughing hysterically. He kept slipping away from me. Mental note: Add running to workout, even though I hate it....a necessary evil. Speaking of which, Cameron's laughter was sounding more and more diabolical by the second. I knew I should put him down before his head started spinning around, Exorcist style.

I finally grabbed him, picked up Courtney, and headed upstairs. He was trying to wriggle free the whole time and he nearly pulled my arm out of its socket. Courtney was easy to put down for a nap. After gathering her stuffed animals around her, she pulled the blanket over her face and said "Goodnight" in a very matter of fact tone.

As for Cameron, I had never seen a mouth open so wide. He was just looking up at me with those hazel eyes of hatred, because I wouldn't let him have another chance at going outside even though he begged. He also wanted a story, which he wasn't getting that day because of his bad behavior. I looked back at him, noticing how his lower lip jutted out, and saw with horror that he had fang teeth on his bottom row. His voice hurt my ears. I peered into that mouth, and just like in cartoons, the punching bag epiglottis at the back of his throat was jumping back and forth, taunting me. Ninja Nanny had no choice. She was going in.

I was having some weird vision in which the epiglottis in Cameron's mouth became the punching bag in my gym, and I, or actually the cartoon version of me, punched and punched on that bag to Eye of the Tiger until I was exhausted. It felt like hours. When I came out of whatever trance this was, he was pulling on my pant leg, yelling "Natalie!"

"Sorry," I said, scooping him up and carrying him towards the bed. Apparently, he'd been trying to get my attention for quite a while.

I had broken a sweat. This wasn't the first time that had happened. It was as if I was exiting my body and going to my happy place. These episodes couldn't continue. I mean, what if I took the kids to gymnastics, and something like this happened, and I broke out in some crescent kicks in public? It just wouldn't do. All those parents would sense something was up, I just knew it. These were only defensive maneuvers—martial arts is not about starting a fight, it's about using self defense only when necessary. I was a natural pacifist anyway and absolutely would never hurt anyone unless I was trying to get them off of me or a loved one. But I had no control over it when this cartoon thing happened. I just froze, and the smack down started in my head.

He was still going to cry. He cried every day at naptime. Yesterday, he screamed my name for 20 minutes in protest. I didn't know how to break him of this. He was already spoiled. I didn't put that there, so I didn't know how to reverse the damage. But he wasn't going to test me constantly and get away with it. I would not let this 3-year-old hellion break me.

I thought and thought about what I could do to make this better. I had to be consistent in my rules and rewards. I constantly had to change it up, distract them so they wouldn't be focused on testing their new nanny. New places worked well for that, as well as not having a predictable routine, and exhausting them as much as possible.

Ninja Nanny needed to strategize.

The Calm Before the Storm

I made chicken parmesan and a big garden salad, and sliced up some asiago cheese bread I'd gotten from the bakery at the market. I surveyed the meal, and it met with my approval, and the caloric intake of a firefighter.

Luckily, it also met with Hammer's. He had a healthy appetite, too. I could tell he was trying not to wolf it down, but was truly starving after a long day of working and working out. "Delicious, Natalie. Thank you." He paused, as if hesitating. "If I may ask, who are the flowers from?"

"Um." This was going to be harder than I'd thought. "They're not from you?"

"Nope," he admitted, looking a little sheepish, and suspicious.

"Well, then I guess they're from someone I met in California."

"Oh really? Wow." He processed this for a moment. "A someone you met who liked you? A someone you met and liked?"

I smiled. "Actually, no… I mean, yes he was really nice to me, and yes, I had the chance, but didn't take it. Didn't want to. I was thinking of someone else at the time, and that someone took up enough space in my heart and head to prevent me from… doing something I would've only regretted."

"I see." I looked at him. Was he upset? Judging by the little smile on his face, he knew I was referring to him, and was happy I had told the truth.

"I didn't exchange contact information with him, so I'm guessing he looked me up." I paused, waiting for him to say something, but he didn't. He just looked at me with those shiny, intense eyes.

"How has this week been for you?" I asked. We were both bare-footed, curled-up facing each other on my big plush couch. Hammer had made a fire in the fireplace.

"It's been pretty productive, actually. We've had some young volunteers coming through our station, and that makes it fun. Teaching them the ropes is cool, and punking them is too."

"Really? What do you do to those poor guys?"

"Well, we change it up each time so the grapevine can't grow through town and ruin the surprise. Sometimes, we initiate the shy ones by having one of the wives ask them to strip and shower in front of them, timed, saying it's part of the protocol. We see how far undressed the guy will get, and then when he's done that, the wife's husband comes out and asks what's going on. The look of utter panic on the newbie's face is worth it. And then we all come out from hiding, keeling over from laughing so hard."

"Sounds like you guys have a lot of fun."

"We sure do. We have ping-pong, a pool table, darts. So on the off hours we have plenty to keep us occupied. It's a good balance for our line of work. Cuts down on stress. Plus, there's job security in firefighting."

I smiled, thinking putting out fires hardly seemed safe and secure. But I knew what he meant. It was a specialized field for remarkable guys, who knew they could lose their lives at any moment. The military signed up for that, but firefighters and cops were in the small number of civilians who did. "Is it what you see yourself doing long term?"

"Maybe. I'm not sure. Sometimes, I want more."

I liked that the big dinner seemed to be loosening him up a little so he would speak frankly to me. "Meaning?"

He smiled. "I want to travel... and help people."

"Okay, so why not do it?"

He sat for a minute, taken aback, considering it. "Well, I guess I could. I've been working for this fire department a few years now."

"All the more reason to change it up, don't you think? It's not good to get stuck, or even feel stuck."

"I agree. Lately I've felt... not stuck in a rut, in a bad way... just stuck in too many routines. Like there's something else I'm supposed to be doing."

I knew exactly what he meant. While he pondered, I excused myself to use the bathroom. I was so enjoying this evening—not only having someone to talk to about life stuff, but the mental stimulation was great. And even beyond that, I felt I could tell this guy just about anything and it would be okay. I wasn't sure how I'd found that out, but I knew I wanted to hold onto the feeling for as long as possible. The added bonus was that he was smokin' hot. It was hard not to get lost in those intense blue eyes. I could swim forever in those. He made me feel safe with his broad shoulders, his strong arms, and knocked me out with his gorgeous smile.

I sat back down on the couch. "Incidentally, Hammer, I may have some knowledge of how you can travel and fight fires and help people."

"You do?"

"Yeah. I have a friend who does it for a living, and I will hook you up with his number." My friend had been helping with forest fires and hurricane aftermath. "He flies to wherever they need him and helps either put out fires, or sometimes just helps people in need. Whatever they're assigned on the trip is what he does, in whatever city they're assigned to go."

"That sounds like exactly what I want to do, Natalie!"

"As much as I'd miss seeing you at the gym, I want you to be happy."

"Thank you. You help me see life in a different way. I've needed that," he said, looking deeply into my eyes, and then he kissed me. Kiki climbed between us and we laughed. She looked up at me, and then at him, with one blue eye and one green.

"Whoa. Cool cat," he said.

"Yeah, she's a phenomenal girl. Sometimes I think she understands what I say, too."

"Well she definitely understands what's going on here tonight."

"What is going on here tonight?" I asked, playing coy.

"Natalie, I really like you. A lot." My heart did somersaults. "When I first saw you, you were doing yoga and I couldn't help noticing what a nice ass you had."

"WHAT?"

"Hehe...just kidding. But seriously." I smacked his arm. "Okay, I'm kidding. The first time I saw you, I was walking out with the guys and you were walking in. I couldn't believe how beautiful you were. You were still in your work clothes and you were wearing a skirt. Your eyes caught mine, and I saw your hair shining and you smiled, sort of shyly. You sure were in a hurry to get in and work out."

"I remember that." My eyes filled with tears that he remembered it, and was sitting there describing it to me. That was over a year ago.

"Sorry about the ass thing. One of the guys actually noticed that part. I did have to agree though," he said, grinning.

I laughed through my tears.

"I notice the person's heart first, and the size of it."

I looked at him for a moment. "Is this your way of telling me you're a chest man? Because I know I don't have a lot in that department…"

"No! I'm really more of a leg man. But that's not what I mean at all. I'm being serious. I can see what's inside a person just by looking at them. I look through the eyes straight into the heart. I could tell instantly that you have a huge heart and that it's very good." He thought a moment. "You, though, Natalie… you have this bad girl thing going on too, and I can't quite put my finger on it, but it's very appealing. It's like, 75% good-hearted woman, 25% vixen. I love that about you."

I smiled. "Thank you." He was very perceptive. Dangerously so. I would have to be careful to hide my secret ninja side… but for my part, I found him irresistible. I loved that he had the balance of being very masculine, but there was no bravado, so he could still show his emotions and be okay with it. We locked eyes, there by the fire, and I pulled him in for another kiss—dessert. ☺ He stood up, bringing me with him, and picked me up so he was holding me against him, fully supporting my body weight. I leaned against his chest. This felt like home. When I was running through the forest in my dream, I'd been running to find this. When I swam at the pool at the gym, I had been swimming trying to feel this. My heart beat to know this. I was emotionally open, for the first time in years. I couldn't let my guard down this way with many people on the planet. Tears flowed from my eyes.

"Are you okay?"

"I get emotional when I eat too much," I said, waving it away, not wanting to explain what I was feeling.

He looked at me. His eyes seemed to find the source of my tears and decipher for himself what was going on. "Beautiful Natalie," he said tenderly. "Always feels she has to make her own way in this world, and does it so well, but inside there's softness."

I hadn't known before that he had this side to him—I liked it. We kissed like this for a few minutes, and I started to laugh.

"Something funny?"

"No, it's just... I was wondering if your arms are getting tired of holding me like this."

"Not at all, Natalie. Not at all. Holding onto you is the best feeling in the world."

He wanted to stay, but had to work the early shift the next morning so he kissed me goodbye, hugged me tightly and left, saying he'd see me soon.

The next morning, I woke up all aflutter. But I wasn't in a crazy rush, I was calm, cool and methodical. It was like everything had come together in my world. I needed his person to center me, and the opposite was also true, of me for him. Two pieces of life's love puzzle had come together. If only every morning could be like this one.

My nanny day got off to a good start too. In order to distract the kids from running around and throwing toys instead of getting dressed, I had them help me make breakfast. We made scrambled eggs, and I had them pour the milk in and help me stir. The thickening process fascinated them. We made pancakes too. Luckily, we didn't have to be anywhere. I let them pour the ingredients, stir the mixture in, and pour into the pan. I told them they could make the pancakes as big or as small as they wanted, so Cam made one the circumference of the pan, and thought it was the most hilarious thing ever. They actually ate the products of our labor, which was another thing the C's wanted me to work on, because typically they didn't eat much.

They loved the structure of the activity. I learned from this and took that ball and ran with it, big time.

After lunch, they had extra energy before it was time to wind down. Instead of going right to story time and trying to fight that energy, I pretended we were in a spaceship. Cameron was the captain, Courtney was co-captain, and I was their passenger. We could stop anywhere they wanted. They decided to shop anywhere they wanted, and went to get clothes at about three different stores. Then they visited Mommy and Daddy at work. After an hour of this, they were ready to take naps. Perfect. They'd be awake and obnoxious again just in time for their parents to get home, and think I wasn't doing my job. I needed more ideas.

While they napped, I took it upon myself to do yoga and some thinking on strategy, to be perfected and executed later.

If they were allowed to use their imagination, they seemed content. The little monsters were transformed into little sweethearts. So I needed activities to encourage their natural creativity and intelligence: activities that bolstered Cameron's confidence and didn't make him feel like he was playing second fiddle to his younger sister; something that made them feel special and really loved.

I looked through the games and craft supplies their mother had bought. There were puzzles, paints, foam letters, coloring books, and magnets. There were stuffed animals galore. There was enough there for a puppet show so I thought I'd create one later on. This would require a special script and a stage. There was construction paper, scissors, stencils. Suddenly, a plan came together. I needed some cardboard boxes, which I didn't find around their house, but I knew I had at mine. I set to work making the hats, and quietly put the other supplies I'd need in my car so I could work on my project overnight.

For today, we could color inside. It was raining out, so I didn't want to risk us all getting colds. I set up the crayons and books, and went to wake them up.

The rest of the day was pretty successful, with a couple minor setbacks. I found I was redefining the word "success." Before, it meant the achievement of something spectacular. Nowadays, it meant getting through the day without anyone getting seriously injured.

Setbacks occurred when I was trying to feed the kids their afternoon snack. They had applesauce, cheese, and crackers. Cameron went into the bathroom and yelled that he needed help. I headed in, but by the time I got to him, there was a puddle of urine about 15 inches from the toilet. My inner dragon fumed. He couldn't have made it the rest of the way to the toilet? Grrr. "Oh Cameron," I said, letting him know I was upset but that it wasn't the end of the world.

"Sorry," he said, trying to help me wipe it up. While we were working, screams came from the kitchen; screams of horror, like someone or something was torturing Courtney. I couldn't leave these kids alone for a split second without them finding trouble. How we could go from peacefully eating a snack to a catastrophic afternoon was beyond me. I ran in there. Somehow, she had knocked over her booster seat and was lying sideways, unable to unstrap herself. I quickly righted her chair, unstrapped her, and picked her up. The wailing continued, directly into my left eardrum. I knew I would need a hearing aid if these kids kept bellowing so close to me. Plus, she was spraying spittle and mucus all over my shoulder. Cameron came and handed me the urine-soaked rag we'd used to clean up his mess.

As I asked him to "please put it in the laundry," my vision closed in from both sides like a curtain closing on a stage, and then re-opened to another reality.

Suddenly I was the cartoon version of me again, and I was punching the bag, over and over, working on my form, my rotation. I knew I was waiting for someone, but I didn't know who. It felt just like that scene in Ghostbusters, with Dan Aykroyd proclaiming, "It just popped in there!" when the Stay Puft Marshmallow Man appeared to them. But I knew my opponent wouldn't be Mr. Stay Puft. I did some kicking combinations, and my challenger hobbled into the dojo, using his cane.

It was Yoda. Somehow, he was the one I had to battle today. At least it wasn't Scooby Doo. I didn't know how I would've fought him, because my love for the famous Great Dane was just too great. But Yoda was a little stud muffin and I appreciated the challenge.

"Ninja Nanny, many challenges you face."

"Indeed, Master Yoda."

"The Force… strong within you, it is. Remember to use it in every situation."

"I shall try."

"Do or do not. There is no try."

I didn't know what to say to that, but I thought it great advice, so I bowed. He bowed too. Then he disappeared. I was secretly thrilled I didn't have to fight the little green grandpa. The truth is I had too much respect for his honor. "I love all your movies," I said, just in case he was still listening from invisible land.

"Thank you, child. Love you, as well, they do," I heard from afar.

I came back to the living room, where I was sitting with the kids. They were laughing at something.

"Natalie, do Yoda again!"

"What?"

"Yoda voice, Yoda voice!" they jumped up and down, tugging at my pant legs. Apparently, I had been speaking his part as well as mine this time. And I had made it to the couch. I hadn't kicked anyone's behind. Maybe these episodes weren't dangerous after all. As long as they didn't happen in public, or while driving.

"I don't think I know how to do Yoda voice."

"But you just did it!"

"Maybe another time, kids," I said. "Let's color. Maybe we'll find a picture of Yoda to color."

"Yeah, maybe! Maybe!"

I sat and watched them color. They got bored after about ten minutes, but I didn't have any energy left. Help me, Obe Wan Kenobi, you're my only hope, I said to myself. I used the force to turn on the TV. Cameron loved TV. Camalia had told me Cameron wasn't to watch more than an hour a day. Courtney got bored with TV, but as long as I played with her every few minutes, she was fine.

I let my energy drain into the couch. I closed my eyes for a minute, and heard a car door open and close.

"Mommy!" the kids said in unison.

I quickly turned off the TV, tiptoed into the kitchen, and grabbed a sponge. I finished wiping up and jumped onto the couch just like Elizabeth Shue in Adventures in Babysitting, hopping over it from behind, grabbing a book from the table and striking a pose. I was calm and collected, as Camalia came in.

She asked how the day went, and I told her really well. I hadn't written about any of the pandemonium in the nanny journal. I guess I believed that if the children were punished for something they'd done five hours ago, or even two, it wouldn't make sense to them. It had to be right in the moment, and that was my job.

In the car, I played some music with a good beat on low volume, and spoke aloud to no one, or maybe to the little jade Buddha on my dashboard:

"At the end of the day, I have gooey, egg-tangled hair, coffee drops instead of tear drops, I'm covered with fluids and solids meant for the toilet but that didn't quite make it. I sweat Captain Crunch-sized beads. My mouth opens and no sound comes out; instead, I hear the screams...the screams of toddlers whose world is ending, who live in the moment, not understanding the concept of time, who insist on accompanying me to the bathroom when duty calls, watching, waiting, wanting to flush the toilet, making comments about what they see there, instructing me not to use too much TP, when they use half a roll each time!

"My brain melts, with nothing but toddler talk for eight hours straight, my body aches from constantly being twisted and turned in all different directions and from them hanging on me. My eyes hurt from trying to overcorrect from not having a pair in the back of my head. The C's are perfectionists, and therefore even if I clean their house from top to bottom, it's never good enough. And, they're raising perfectionists, and I find myself unable to do a damn thing about it! And on top of it all, I must be losing my mind, because I just met Yoda."

I waited, and got no response from Buddha or anyone else for that matter. That's okay, because I felt better anyway. Everyone should have something in their car that makes them feel good, no matter what the surrounding drivers are doing. I rubbed the Buddha belly for luck. "Thanks for listening." I wasn't a Buddhist, but I had studied it some and the beliefs tended to match my own. I liked how much they respected nature and believed in getting energy and power from it, and in giving back.

At home, I set about making something that, with any luck, would enchant and delight the little munchkins, and drifted off listening to ambient music playing from online.

In the morning, I folded the seats down in my Escape and put my creation inside. My windows were tinted of course, so I didn't have to worry about them seeing it before it was time.

We made it through getting dressed, breakfast, and dropping Cameron off at school—I used the family Land Cruiser for all kid-related driving because it had the kid seats in it. I could feel people thinking, Soccer mom, all the way, when they looked at me. I smiled secretly, to think how I was leading a double life—no one knew I was a secret ninja, except my trainer, the others in the class, and Sam. But she didn't know any details. I told her I couldn't disclose that information, so she knew not to ask. It was almost breaking the rules that she knew I did it in the first place. However, unlike most people I'd met, she was trustworthy.

I took Courtney to the store where we did the family's shopping, and we looked at the lobsters in the tank. It was easier than going to the aquarium, and she was mesmerized for quite a while in front of that tank. When she started to squirm, we moved to the crab tank. It looked like one of them was waving at us, so we waved back at his pincer. We had a snack, and I took her to the library and read her a story. She actually paid attention to it. After that, it was time to pick up Cameron.

On the way home, Cameron asked me where we went. Then he asked why. Why we went to the store, why we went to the library, why we didn't take him. I fell into the trap of answering those questions at first, and then he kept asking why questions, which was threatening to drive me insane, so I just turned the stereo up and stayed quiet. It didn't work. He just raised his voice. Pretty soon, his sister followed suit. "Why?" "Why?" "Natalie, why?" "Natalieee, whyyy?"

"Why why why why why why why why?"

I tried to distract them. "What would you like for lunch?"

"Chicken nuggets!" they said in unison. That's what they always wanted. I hadn't served those yet and didn't plan on it. This was more of the behavior I didn't put there, and didn't know how to get rid of.

"How about you can have peanut butter and jelly sandwiches."

"No! Chicken nuggets!"

"You can have peanut butter sandwiches, or you can have sautéed monkey brains."

"Peanut butter! Peanut butter!" they said through laughter.

"Can we go see the Lollipop Man?" Cameron asked.

"Not today, Cam. Natalie doesn't want coffee today." Such a fib—but I had to make it a special reward for being extra good. "If you're on extra-super-duper-magnificent behavior, maybe you can see the Lollipop Man sometime this week." I could tell they were considering it, quietly there in the backseat, so I asked what good behavior was, and they shot off some decent definitions. They finally started speaking gibberish, so I started thinking about how cool it was that I'd taken control of the situation instead of going to my happy place this time—especially since I was driving. Plus, who knew next time what might show up? Last time it was Yoda, this time it could be the Hulk. I didn't think I was quite ready to battle him.

I fixed them peanut butter and jelly sandwiches, and gave them extra potato chips. The kids were so skinny, it looked like they never ate at all. Cameron ate well today, but afterwards, ran around with one hand on each of my butt cheeks as I did the dishes. "I'm touching your butty, I'm touching your butty!"

"Cameron, stop! That's not appropriate behavior."

He was running wild, still yelling it, and would not let go. I was really glad the neighbors couldn't hear us. I thought about pretending to call the police, but I didn't have the energy. I asked him to help me put Courtney to bed. "As long as I can touch your butty!"

"First of all, the word is 'booty,' and no, you may not touch it. If you continue, no story today before nap."

"Okay. I stop touching your butty."

"Booty. Thank you." I turned around to put Courtney in her crib.

Slap! "I spank your booty! HAHAHAHAHAAA!"

"Cameron, that's it. No story." It was as if I'd said, *Ladies and gentlemen, let the wailing begin!* His screams and cries sounded as though I had literally taken away his birthday. He ran into his room and slammed the door.

"I don't love nobody, I just love Wanda!" Wanda was the cat. It was the biggest, furriest black cat I'd ever seen. It looked like someone had put it through the spin cycle and then teased its hair and finished off by spraying some Aqua Net up in there too. To top it all off, Wanda was a boy. Yet the cat was Cameron's beloved friend, who slept at the foot of his bed almost every day.

In between wails, I read Courtney her story, and she managed to drift off to sleep with her brother still sounding like a foghorn in the next room. I was beat, but went downstairs to clean the kitchen and play area, and listened for Cameron. His cries were subsiding. Five minutes of silence went by, and finally, finally he was finished with this outburst.

I ran the mini-vac over the carpet to get all the tufts of black cat hair out, and started setting up my surprise. By the time I finished, I had just enough time for a 15-minute power nap before I woke the kids. So I set the alarm on my cell phone, and snoozed deeply. I woke up, shook it off and went to wake up Courtney and changed her diaper, and then woke up Cameron. He had gone to sleep on top of his blankets, in his school clothes with his shoes still on, and was delighted to still be dressed. He kept showing us that he was still dressed. By the eighth "Look Natalie, look Courtney, I still have my shoes on!" I was ready to distract him, so we walked downstairs.

Cameron was always a couple steps ahead of the rest of the world, with all his excess energy, and Courtney was always a couple steps behind, at least on the stairs, which she hadn't mastered just yet. Cameron stopped on the landing and gasped. He looked up at me, and to his sister. "Guys, look!"

"What is it, Cam?" I said, all excited anticipation.

Courtney took a deep breath, and a "Wow!" exploded out of her as she met him on the landing.

Before us, a pirate ship filled up nearly the whole living room, from end to end. It was made of cardboard, but I had put gold and purple construction paper on it, and the trim was made of green streamers. I had created a sail out of some straightened coat hangers and lots of paper towels, and it shined with purple and gold glitter. The only part I had bought was the pirate flag, from the dollar store—they had tons of cool stuff because Halloween was coming up in a month. In the bottom of the ship, there was a door for Cameron, and a door for Courtney, to match each of their respective heights. At either end of the ship, turquoise and blue waves splashed up, making whitecaps. I had even put a mermaid on the bow of the boat. That's what took me the longest. She had long blond hair, strategically placed shells, and was winking at the kids.

I went to the kitchen, pulled pirate hats and scarves out of a drawer, and put them on the kids (including one of each for me, of course). "You are now both officially pirates of the South Seas."

"Ahoy, matey!" I said to Cameron.

He turned and said, "Ahoy, matey!" to his sister, who turned and said, "Ahoy, matey!" to me.

"Swab the deck!" I said, handing them each a miniature mop. (Okay, I bought those from the dollar store, too. They were the old-fashioned stringy kind).

The kids played in the ship until Mommy and Daddy got home. We pretended pirates were coming to get us (the not-so-scary, Johnny Depp type pirates) and to steal our treasure, which was in a chest the family had, and it looked exactly like it should - filled with gold and jewels, in our imaginations. I'm sure the C's didn't have a clue what they were going to do with the ship when guests came over, but I suggested showing it off to neighbors and parents, which not only got me out of figuring out the answer to that question, but was an underhanded way of promoting my services as a babysitter. Cameron and Courtney didn't want me to leave that day. Finally, things were improving. I hoped the kids' testing of me would lessen at least somewhat now.

I decided to do something special for the kids the next day, just because.

At breakfast, Cameron was teaching his sister how to wear her breakfast bowl on her head. They were done eating cereal, but neither one drank all the milk, so they both had it running down their hair and faces and the rest of them. Luckily, I had let them eat breakfast without getting dressed this morning so we only had to get dressed once. I waited until they finished acting out, until they had all the deviant behavior out of their systems for the time being. Then I'd clean up their faces. I'd let them live in their milky, wet pajamas for a while. Maybe, just possibly, the memory of this would teach them a little something. When enough time had passed, I threw them both into the shower, rinsed them off and let them wash each other's hair. They both got shampoo in their eyes, so the lesson of never wearing cereal and milk again was learned. I didn't plan it that way, but it ended up working out.

The chaos continued, however, as we returned to the downstairs. Cameron wasn't content to play a game with his sister while I finished the fine details of kitchen cleaning, so he crawled up into the breakfast booth, moved his little seat over to the wall so I couldn't reach it, and stood up on the arm of it. "Cameron, you're going to fall. Please get down," I said.

"No," he said laughing and bouncing a little bit.

"Yes," I said. "You think this is funny now, but if you fall it will hurt. Please."

"Nope," he said, shaking his head in glee.

And then he fell. And all hell broke loose. He cried and screamed for fifteen minutes. I comforted him, wiped his tears and checked for scrapes. There were none. Then I tackled their mess and assorted other remnants from last night's dinner. Seeing the mop and broom, Cameron got excited. He started dancing around, and I went and turned the television on. He was in TV land—for about five minutes. He came back and jumped around in the mop water on the floor.

"Cameron, please! I don't want you to fall." Right then, he fell. This time, he was more shocked than hurt, and he hugged my leg, saying he was sorry. I had my hand on his little head. I was so worried about this boy. When he threw himself into a frenzy, he heard nothing, and he would hurt his sister if she was in the way. Fortunately, she was still quietly playing her game. The only thing I could think of to do was to distract their minds.

"Mars to planet Cam-Ron. Mars to Cam-Ron. Come in, Cam-Ron." He was surprised, as he'd never heard me speak in alien monotones before. "Mars to planet Court-On-Eee. Mars to Court-On-Eee." They finally jumped onboard my spaceship and started talked in alien monotones too. I was pleased with myself. I still had to build them a spaceship, but that would be for later when the pirate ship had lost its magic. We had an imaginary one, and flew upstairs in it to pick up Cam-Ron's clothes and then Court-On-Eee's. "Come on, kidlets. We're going to the gym of Nat-A-Leee," I continued in monotone alien voice. I needed a workout in the worst way after this morning.

We got to the gym, and the fire engine wasn't there. That was okay, because I didn't need Hammer and his buddies laughing at my attempt to control the kids. All I had to do was get them upstairs safely into the Kids' Club room, but some days even that seemed hard. I had them hold my hands in the parking lot, but Cameron yanked away from me and almost got hit by a car. Almost. I didn't know what to do with this kid! Even my best attempts to ensure his safety weren't enough. He needed a kid leash. His parents said they didn't like those, but I was thinking of investing in some anyway and using them in secret.

I'd been considering taking them out to lunch, but I was going to save that for next week. Good behavior was to be rewarded, not bad. So today we might get to see the Lollipop Man at the Lollipop Stand, if they were on superlative behavior for the rest of the day.

I walked in, put the kids on the seats at the door's entrance, directly behind me, as usual. There was heavy foot traffic at the door, and if I told them to stand by me, they usually wandered away after about 30 seconds and got under people's feet. I checked myself in, told Jeremy, the guy at the front desk, "Two for Kids' Club," and started to hand him the money. All of a sudden, I heard the fire alarm go off. Was there really a fire? I asked Jeremy where it came from. He smiled slightly, and pointed to the kids. Oh no they didn't, I thought. I turned around. Oh, yes they had.

Cameron was half smiling. He had this look that I read as, I'm going to pay hell for this, but I am so proud that this drama all happening because of me. I gave him the evil eye that said, you're right, you are going to get it. I wanted him to be scared. Courtney just looked worried like she didn't know what was going on. She looked at her brother and smiled too, until his smile quickly faded while he studied my face, and turned into a look of fear. Mission accomplished. She followed his gaze to my face and immediately stopped smiling. I put my head in my hands for a second. By this time, all the personal trainers in the club had come from wherever they were in the building, to the front desk, asking where the owner was, asking if there was really a fire. I read their lips, because it was so loud. The owner wasn't there yet. All the older ladies came down the stairs and filed out of the club in their swimsuits.

Apparently, they needed the owner to unlock the room with the switch in it, to turn off the alarm. He was the only one who had the key. The firefighters were already on their way. Sweet Jesus. "I'm so sorry!" I mouthed to Jeremy. He just smiled. All I could think of to do was blend in, so I grabbed the kids' hands, and filed outside with the rest of the, oh, I'd say 250 people who were in the gym that morning. I stood there and gave Cameron the biggest lecture of his life. Talk about punishing him in the moment.

I wanted to just leave the club, right then and there. I was just that mortified. However, it would have been the cowardly way, and that was not mine. In addition, the members blocked in the car, and the fire trucks were coming around the corner. I stopped lecturing Cameron, who was enjoying this too much to care what I was saying. To him, it was all a big party in the parking lot that he had started, and when he heard the sirens, he was even more delighted. I didn't cry, but I was feeling very anxious. My stomach churned. One engine, one truck, and one ambulance were now parked in front of the building. The fire station was just across the street from my gym, so by the time Jeremy had called them, it was too late. They ran inside, in full gear. Now, I was crying. I couldn't even tell which one was Hammer.

Five minutes later, I could tell which one was Hammer. He and the guys were laughing as they walked out the door. They held the door open for all of the older ladies, who filed back inside in their bathing suits and towels. Poor things, a couple of them were starting to look a little blue. If any of them caught pneumonia and died from this, I wouldn't be able to forgive myself. Or Cameron. *Ever.*

Hammer had figured out that I was the one with the kids who had committed this act, or someone had told him. He was walking toward the fire engine he'd been driving, but his eyes were scanning the crowd for me. Before he could spot me, I ran inside with the kids and locked all three of us in the big handicapped bathroom. I wanted to hide in there until the gym closed and everyone went home, but I knew I couldn't—surely, people would have to use the bathroom in the next 12 hours. Right now, I had to though. I told Cameron we weren't going out to lunch today because he had pulled the fire alarm. He looked at me as solemnly as possible, but I could tell he was proud of his actions and the world's reactions and would wear that badge until the day he died. There was not much I could do about it, except move on, and not linger in the moment and give this kid any reinforcement, for he even seemed to thrive on the negative kind. Cameron was obviously ecstatic about it, though. Sigh.

I heard a knock on the door. "Be right out," I said. There was muffled laughter on the other side of the door.

"Is Naughty Natalie in there?"

"No."

"Oh, I think she is!"

Craptastic. I had to open the door. I took a deep breath and opened the door. Four firefighters and an EMT stood there, and as I looked at all of them, they gave me a standing ovation. It was the most humiliating moment of my life. I felt like I'd done something really, really bad in school and it was the moment of punishment which could not be avoided at any cost. I tried to walk around them and through them, but Hammer was heading up the team, and he held me in place. The kids and I weren't going anywhere.

"Natalie, I hereby present you with the award for "Best Fake Fire Ever." He took out of his pocket a tiny toy fireman hanging on a chain, put it around my neck, and then got down on his knees and did the worship bow. The rest of the firefighters clapped again. Gym members were standing around, trying to get a glimpse of what was happening. My face turned several different shades, including puce, magenta, burgundy, scarlet, and crimson. Hammer then asked which of the kids had pulled the fire alarm. Cameron gleefully admitted guilt, and Hammer asked if he could borrow Cameron for a minute.

"Sure," I said. I didn't want to give Cameron the impression he was being punished by a man and not by me, but I had really tried to get through to him, and he just didn't respond to my punishments the same way. I had seen

89

the same thing happen with his mom and dad when they got home, so I didn't feel too badly about that. Plus, it might mean a little more coming from a firefighter in his gear.

We all went to the door, and with a very serious face, Hammer told Cameron never to pull that handle unless there was an actual fire or smoke that looked dangerous, because there might be another real fire somewhere else, and people could die. So it was very important for firefighters not to waste their time on a pretend call. A wide-eyed Cameron understood, and agreed. They shook hands. Astounding.

I thanked Hammer, apologized profusely, and we left. "I'll call you soon," he said as we walked away. I smiled and waved but didn't answer—my nerves were too frazzled by that point. I was exhausted, so took the kids to McDonald's drive-through, and explained to them that this was not a treat. I knew my words weren't really reaching them as they happily ate their Happy Meals, but I was too tired to care at this point.

We got home and Cameron asked when we were going to a sit down restaurant. I told him maybe next week if he was on very good behavior. I let them work off some energy outside before naptime. They didn't fight me today on going to sleep—I guess they figured they'd maxed out their quota for bad behavior. I fell asleep on the couch for an hour and a half and dreamed of putting out the fires that the Stay Puft Marshmallow Man was setting, with Yoda's help extinguishing them. When I woke up, I was still tired.

That night, Hammer called. Before I could say anything, he told me it was okay about what happened, and that he and the guys had had a good laugh over it that lasted all day long.

"Thanks for making me feel better," I said.

"Did you tell the C's?"

"No. I felt it was best to let it lie, so to speak, because Cameron would get more attention for what he did, and consider it a good thing. He understood your lecture today; that was enough."

"Do you think he'll tell his parents?"

"Yes, but I'm thinking they'll think he made it up. If they don't, I'll tell them later. I didn't lie and tell them their kids were perfect today, I just said it was a pretty long day, in the nanny journal."

"You have to keep a journal?"

"Yep."

"Mmhm."

"Yeah, I know. If I wrote half of what actually went on in there, they would fire their kids and get some new ones." He laughed.

"I have news," he announced.

"What is it?"

"I called your friend about the job. He put me in contact with the company and they want to meet me."

"Really? How exciting!"

"Yeah, I fly out to Nevada tomorrow to interview."

"Wow, they waste no time!"

"I know. Which means I want to see you either tonight or as soon as I get back."

"How about as soon as you get back? I don't have much energy left for anything tonight."

"I kind of thought that's what you'd say, so I was going to offer to bring you some dinner."

"Really?" My heart did that swelling and melting thing that hearts do when someone is too wonderful for words. "You're not too busy packing and getting ready?"

"Already done."

"Wow, you're good. Okay. Give me time to hop in the shower and wash off the day."

"You got it. I'll be over in… how about an hour and a half?"

"Cool. See you then."

I went directly into the shower without passing go or collecting $200 and washed off all the worries and tears, and had just finished getting ready when the doorbell rang. I opened the door, and there was who I thought was Hammer, standing behind a huge bouquet of roses. There were purple ones, yellow ones, deep read ones, and white ones. There must have been 12 of each color—and a few blue thrown in as well. It must have cost a fortune. "How beautiful!"

The roses were handed to me, and I saw that it wasn't Hammer. "Here you go, ma'am," said a teenage delivery boy.

"Thank you…" I looked around for a delivery card, and there wasn't one, so I asked, "Who are they from?"

"There is a card hidden somewhere in there," he said, and gave me a shy smile and skulked away to the delivery van.

"Thanks!" I said to his back.

I found the card. "To Natalie: We all enjoyed meeting you today, and wish you the best of luck with those kids! What a handful." It was from the guys at the fire department. I was so touched, and I felt very undeserving of these flowers.

Hammer arrived minutes later, ringing the bell. This time, I knew it had to be him, and it was. I greeted him by running and jumping into his arms. Unfortunately, my jump was a little forceful and almost knocked him over. He laughed anyway and kissed me hello, spinning me around on the sidewalk outside my apartment. He put me down, and I headed in. He picked up dinner, which luckily he had set down outside. He had brought pizza, and the smell wafted to my nostrils.

"Yum!"

"I hope you like meat lovers' because that's what I got."

"Perfect. So, what's behind your back?"

"Well, I see the guys beat me to it, but here you go." He brought out a bouquet of wildflowers. They also had lilies in them. "I couldn't let the department outdo me."

I smiled, thanked him and said, "You all better stop with the flowers. It's beginning to look like someone died in here." He laughed, and I said I was kidding just in case he got the idea I didn't like flowers, because I really wouldn't want to ever give him that idea. I gave him another huge hug.

"If you keep doing that, we'll have to skip dinner," he said. So I laughed, but I kept doing it, and we skipped dinner and had cold pizza for dessert by the fire. We were wrapped in blankets. I had never had this much fun in one month in my entire life. From the trip until now, my life was exactly how I wanted it to be. I had finally found a good guy... an amazing guy. And he was leaving. Because I had hooked him up with how to leave. I was really happy for him, but I'd miss him a lot. I guess my face showed my emotions.

"I won't be gone that long. Even if I get the job, I'll be here on weekends as much as possible."

"Thanks for saying that. It's just..."

"Yeah, I know. We just found each other."

"Yeah."

He just held me, and we looked at the fire together for a long time.

On Monday, I took the kids out to eat after picking Cam up from preschool. We went to a nice family-style restaurant that was not part of a chain.

"Where are we going? Where are we going?" I just smiled as they asked this over and over from the backseat.

"It's a surprise."

When we got there, Court asked, "What's this restaurant called, Natalie?"

"The Steakhouse Grill. Have you ever been here?"

"No."

We were seated and I read the kid menus to them. They wanted chicken nuggets, but those weren't on the menu, so I suggested some other entrees. Court decided on a grilled cheese sandwich and fries, and Cam a burger and fries. I had them order for themselves.

Cam said, "I'll have a hangaber."

Court ordered a, "gwilled cheese with fwies."

I asked the server to have their meals cut up into little pieces, and I ordered a blackened chicken salad and a side of fries. Hey, I wanted to enjoy my meal too. The server asked if the kids wanted some crayons, and they both said yes.

"Yes what?"

"Yes please."

"Good. Sure, bring them some crayons, please. Thanks."

They proceeded to drop, break and/or throw every crayon onto the floor, despite my warnings that we would go home without eating lunch. Once they were all on the floor, I wouldn't help them pick the crayons up, so Cameron got under there and did it, also finding French fries and putting those on the table next to the crayons. All I could see was his hand, which was rather amusing as the fries kept coming. "Nice job, Cameron. Now put the fries in the garbage and see if you can keep the crayons all on the table."

"Okay." They did pretty well with that, only dropping a couple. I was happy so far. Then Cameron stood up on his seat and refused to sit down.

"Cam, remember what happened when you did that at home?"

"I fell."

"That's right, you fell. Please sit down. I don't want you to get hurt again." After a few more requests, he sat down, but was squirming. Inside, I was squirming, horrified that people might get the idea these were my children. It often happened, because Courtney had big almond-shaped eyes like mine, so people made assumptions. I wouldn't have minded them assuming I had kids. Just sometimes...not these particular ones.

"I have to go poopy," Cameron proclaimed, at the top of his lungs while standing back up on his seat. So we all went to accompany him. Luckily, there was a big restroom and we could all fit in it easily. He did his business, and I wiped his bottom as I always did until he learned to do it himself. Oh how I enjoyed doing this. By enjoyed of course I meant loathed. Especially when all I wanted to do was have a nice lunch, go home, and put them to bed.

We got back to the table, as the food came.

Courtney put all of her grilled cheese chunks onto her napkin, rolled it into a ball, and squished it together. "Mmmm, gwilled cheese ball!" I tried hard to suppress my laughter at her new recipe. She dug in, and had grease and cheese all over her face by the time she was done. This family should buy stock in baby wipes.

Cameron threw all his silverware on the floor, and then reached over for Courtney's.

"Cameron, that's enough! Bad manners get reported to Mommy and Daddy, remember?"

He put her fork down and gave me a devious smile, like he'd do it the minute my back was turned. I made sure not to turn it this time.

A woman sitting across from us said "Such lovely children. And *so* well behaved."

"Thanks. I'll tell their parents you said so," I said, wondering from which planet I could acquire some of the particular rose-colored glasses she was wearing. I sure as h-e-double hockey sticks didn't see any well behaved children at this table.

On the way out the door, they asked if they could have some candy from the machine, and I said yes. I just didn't want to hear the screaming and crying when they didn't get the one little thing their precious hearts desired. Boy did they have me trained well—at least after they had already been behaving poorly all day. My head started to pound.

"Ready to go home and take naps?"

"Can we play in the pirate ship first?"

"Yes, for 15 minutes." This seemed to satisfy them, and I didn't hear any whining. I put the windows down and they went Woohoo, all the way home.

I changed things up, and sang Courtney a song instead of telling her a story, and I had Cameron tell me a make believe story instead of me reading him one. His bedtime story collection (all of ten total) had gotten old, and I hadn't had a chance to sift through my own from when I was little, to widen his selection. He made up a story about a dragon and a little boy who were friends. The little boy had to become a firefighter to be the dragon's friend and avoid getting charred. He told me then that he wanted to be a firefighter when he grew up. I wasn't sure how his parents would feel about that choice, being go-getter types who would likely want their son to be president someday, but at least the boy had goals, which was pretty impressive for three years old. I was sure it would change a few times anyway depending on what was going on in his life.

He had trouble going to sleep that day. His mind was on dragons and fires, so I rubbed his temples and told him softly to relax.

Later we went for a bike ride around the neighborhood, as we had for countless afternoons. Courtney wanted her bike first, but after about two blocks, she got tired and walked. Her walking pace was really slow, so I picked her up and carried her in one hand and her bike with my other. This left Cameron riding way ahead of us. I kept yelling at him to slow down, and he ignored me. I wasn't too worried because he knew how to look both ways to check for traffic, but yelled out a warning, just in case.

When we got back to the house, we put the bikes back in the garage, and I told them it was time to come inside. I turned toward the back entrance and walked two steps. I heard fast footsteps behind me going the other way, so I turned around. Cameron ran in one direction, and Courtney ran in the other. I didn't know which way to run first, so I went after Courtney who didn't know how to look for traffic and stop in time. By the time I got to her, Cameron was running toward the road at breakneck pace, and wouldn't stop when I yelled, over and over. He just turned and laughed, acting as if it were a game, and completely wild and out of control.

I knew I couldn't possibly physically reach him, even if I ran as fast as I could. "Cameron! Cameron, stop!" He didn't. I closed my eyes, focused, and inexplicably got to him right before he reached the road, and right before a bus would've hit his little body. I scooped him up and ran to the sidewalk.

"Cameron," I said, through tears and out of breath.

"What, Natalie?" he laughed until he saw tears running down my face. "What's wrong?"

"Cameron, you could have been killed by that bus." I let that sink in, waiting until I saw him process the word "killed." "Please, please don't ever run away from me like that again." All I wanted to do was go inside and sit down, so I kept walking, holding his hand and carrying her. Courtney was very wide-eyed and kept asking me what was wrong. When we got inside, I sat down on the couch and waited until they were both directly in front of me, giving me their full attention. Silence works wonders when a kid knows something is up. Cameron listened attentively, nodding that he understood me.

"But Natalie, how did you catch me?"

"What do you mean?"

"I mean, you didn't run. I too far away. You just come there." He was struggling with his words, but I knew what he meant. I smiled. He sure didn't miss anything.

"Cam, I ran so fast you couldn't see me."

He studied me for a moment, knowing something else had happened. But luckily, his 3-year-old attention span just wouldn't let him dwell on it. Courtney was taking it all in and just looked at me in wonder for the rest of the afternoon. She, after all, had been in my arms when I disappeared and reappeared, taking that journey with me.

"Listen, kids. This is very serious. I don't want to tell your Mommy and Daddy what happened today, but I have to."

"Why?"

"Because if you run away from me, you could get hurt. If you run in one direction and you run in the other, I can't catch both of you at the same time. I don't want you to get hurt or die, so you have to mind me."

"Mind you outside?" Cameron asked.

"Mind me outside and inside, because you can get hurt inside too. Remember when you fell in the kitchen, Cam?"

"Yes."

"Did that hurt?"

"Yes."

"That's right. Were you minding when that happened?"

"No. I was being bad boy."

"Yes, you were being bad. How about today when you ran away?"

"I bad. I bad I bad I bad!!!" I waited until he was done marching around in a little circle bellowing it.

"You know how to be on good behavior, Cameron."

"I know."

"How could you have been better today?"

He paused, eyes rolling up, and put his hand in his hair, scratching his head. "Um...I.....I.....coulda listened Natalie."

"That's right! You should have listened to Natalie. Why?"

The lecture went on for a few more minutes this way. Thankfully, it was almost time for the C's to get home, so I turned on the TV and set about straightening up, and then wrote about what happened in the journal, minus the disappearing part. I was more than happy to leave. Today had just been too taxing, and I had to try to figure out what had happened.

Testing—One, Two, Three. Testing...

With Hammer gone, I had nothing better to do than throw myself into my training. I had asked my teacher to give me some extra hard challenges, because balance was key, and I needed enough objectives to both keep me on my game, and keep my mind off of work. He obliged.

I laughed as I approached the dojo door. There was a wooden sign, "Chi Club Challenge" just inside the main entrance. Apparently he'd done this for students before—either that or he had a sign-making shop somewhere in here I didn't know about. That would be my trainer's sense of humor. He'd do something like that to loosen me up. He always told me to relax into it, not to be tense before sparring.

I looked around and saw that he'd set up an obstacle course. I couldn't enter the dojo if I couldn't get through the course. It was like something from a movie. The hallway leading up to the door was filled with equipment he had borrowed from the gym that I had to climb over, shimmy under, and balance on. Some of it moved and swung, and I had to drop and roll to avoid being hit. It was so cool, like going into the Temple of Doom.

I entered my code and stepped inside, sure that the challenge wasn't over. I bowed as I saw him come out a door diagonal to where I stood. He bowed, walked to me and greeted me with a kali, fighting stick, handed me mine, and we used them for 20 minutes. This part made me feel like I was in the Matrix Reloaded, the scene where Neo had to fight a stranger before finding out the man's identity.

We did hand to hand combat, and I threw punches and back fists and blocked nearly every one of his. "Now, only kicks!" he directed. I did front kicks, side kicks, back kicks, crescent kicks, a roundhouse kick, and a jump spinning wheel kick. The last one was new to me, but I did a successful one, which pleased both of us.

I didn't have to break wood this time, but I was feeling pretty winded from spending an hour fighting what I hadn't known was coming.

"Congratulations, Phoenix. Today, you faced the tiger."

"Thank you, Sifu." We bowed and I left. He never expected me to help set up or take down, and I appreciated that. I didn't know if he was doing the same things with other students, but I had enough prep to do for work so I didn't wish to do it here. I always asked him if he needed help taking gear down, and he always said no. I wanted to ask him about what'd happened to me at work that day, but didn't want to interrupt his busy schedule more than my training already did.

While driving home, I thought about The Way, which was not a specific path with signs to direct me, but a way of life, a lifestyle. Martial artists tried not to be attached to things, in life, because attachment created pain. People and situations were temporary, and too much emotional attachment was not good. The feeling of ownership that most people had over others was not healthy. I was trying to adhere to this as much as possible with Hammer. I didn't want to own him, but I did want to enjoy being with him as much as possible. I wanted him to find his own happiness. That was The Way. Even if he ended up breaking up with me, if he found inner peace and happiness, instead of wallowing in self-pity, I would be happy for him. My love for him was as pure and true as could be. I hoped he would get this job, so his soul would shine with joy. I was just happy to have felt the feeling he caused me to feel. It wasn't easy to evolve to this manner of thinking, because of my fondness for Virgos, and more specifically, for that Virgo. However, what my trainer had taught me was finally clicking in. The choice was easy: either live in eternal agony of wanting things to be exactly how you want them, or roll with it. Rolling with it was much more beneficial for all. Now that I had arrived there in my head, I couldn't think of leaving. It made life a lot easier not to always be wanting more—and to just 'be'.

I got home, and there was a message, but not from Hammer. It was from Sam. She was calling to report that the weekend with Marty had been amazing. He was thinking of moving to Washington to be with her.

"And break up the brotherly love of the California firefighters?" I asked, calling her back.

"Apparently. Their town isn't big enough for both their egos," she laughed.

"Ha! You called that one."

"So how's Hammer?"

"I haven't heard from him since he left for the interview. I assume they're busy testing his skills."

"I know he'll get it."

"Me too."

"Are you sad?"

"Not at all. I'm thrilled. I just want him to do what he truly wants to, because you know what? Life is not worth it if you can't do what you love."

"I so agree."

"Plus, I've always valued my alone time, as you know."

"Hehe… you haven't told him about martial arts yet, have you?"

"Nah. I thought I'd save that one for later."

"After there's an engagement ring on your finger?"

"No! You know I'm not conniving like that and I resent women who are. They give the genuine girls like us a bad name. I just need to find the right time to tell him about my ninja-by-night self. He opened the door to discussion last time, but I wasn't ready to step through it."

"He hasn't looked in your closet and seen your after hours wardrobe, eh?"

"You're funny. Actually, I don't have one. That's just so Hollywood." In this case, what she didn't know couldn't hurt her. Literally. I didn't have any kinky stuff in my spare closet, just a bunch of martial arts gear.

My trainer and I sat facing each other in a Japanese garden. We drank tea, which tasted like orange and vanilla with a little cinnamon sprinkled in. I felt serene.

I was dressed in a white robe with a sash around the middle. He was dressed in a black yoga suit. There was a fountain with Japanese characters carved in stone on the ground around it, and music was playing, but it wasn't Japanese. It was some kind of ambient music with ocean sounds. On the other hand, maybe it was ambient music and I was really hearing the ocean. But I didn't see or smell salt water.

"Greetings, my student. I feel you have questions for me," he said, smiling.

"Hello, trainer. Yes, I do."

"Good. You can call me Jin. It is my real name."

"Okay."

"I called this meeting so that we could communicate and commune. I know this is needed. I know you don't feel you have enough time with me at the gym, and so I have created this space; it's a sanctuary of sorts, where we can talk without interruption or distraction."

"Thank you, trainer Jin."

"What is it that troubles you?"

"Well… I don't understand what's happening to me."

"Go on."

"You know that I'm a nanny." He nodded. "Lately, whenever the kids are being bad, and I mean very... beyond my control bad, I go somewhere else."

"You mean you escape into the mind?"

"Yes. I temporarily exit the scene, and suddenly I'm fighting or talking with someone in the dojo. It lasts for several minutes that I know of, and then I come back. I'm scared, because this never happened before I started this job and I don't want to endanger the kids."

"Is there anything else you can tell me about these episodes?"

"Well, just that they have never happened in public, at least while surrounded by too many people. And sometimes I'm the cartoon version of myself."

"I see. Do you have any idea why this is happening now?"

"No. That's why I wanted your help."

"Has anything else happened?"

"Yes."

"I will need to know about it in order to help you."

"Okay." I described Cameron and Courtney running in opposite directions, and that I disappeared and saved Cameron from being hit by a bus.

"Aaaaah," he said. "Now I understand. You were being built up to that point, where you would save the child."

"You mean the other experiences were a sort of training for that moment?"

"Yes. It is a rare talent you have. Firstly, to be able to disappear like you did. Only a handful people in the world, all martial artists, have mastered this skill. Secondly, the reason you were able to master it was, you use your talents for the greatest possible good. It's a purity which enables you to step beyond the limitations of time and space to do a noble deed." He surveyed me, making sure I was getting what he was telling me.

"Have you done it?"

"Yes. That is how I know. My teacher also explained it to me, shortly after it happened."

"Did I create the counter-reality that I went to in these episodes?"

"No. You were pulled in by those who came before you. They were testing your stamina, your spirit, your grace."

"Just by talking to me, watching me fight?"

"Yes."

"Is who I see during an episode controlled by those who came before me?

"No. You'll bring in who you need to see, speak to, or spar with based on what your mind considers appropriate."

"The time you prepared special challenges for me, was this real?"

"Both what you experience in your mind's dojo, and in my dojo are real. But I did this for you at the gym studio, yes."

"Thank you. I thought I was losing it there for a minute."

"There is no danger of that, my dear girl. You are on solid ground."

I smiled. "Do you think this will happen to me in the future?"

"I don't know the answer to that. I can't talk about the future, only the past and present. If you need to commit further heroic acts and need guidance, you will receive it. You can request that it happen at a time that you won't be harmed, such as sleeping. You can request that it never happen to you while driving, for instance, or in public. The requests that make sense to those who've gone before will be honored."

"I see. Will I remember it, if it happens while I'm sleeping?"

"You may not remember it; like some dreams, it may be forgotten...but you will absorb and retain the knowledge."

"I have one more question."

"Shoot."

"Will I remember meeting you and talking to you here?"

"If you wish. It is *all* up to you. You can come back here any time you need to, and whenever I can, I will meet you. Summon me by using our signal, and I will hear you."

And with that, he disappeared, leaving only sand swirling around him. I woke up smiling, because I remembered the whole thing.

And then I looked at the clock, and grimaced. There was never enough time in the morning. I should've asked him if I could fix that too. Make each minute of the morning before work five times as long, so I could wake my brain up before leaving. I wondered what those who came before me would say to that. I...I...I...I...want more tiiime, I thought, thinking it like Eddie Murphy in the Golden Child and cracking myself up. I was sure that those who had to start work early everywhere would thank me for it.

I rushed around getting ready, and on the way out the door noticed my answering machine flashing. It was Hammer. "Hey, babe. Guess what... I got the job!" I jumped for joy, both that he had gotten the job and that he'd used that term to refer to me. I did said jump while still inside my apartment, so my neighbors didn't think I was just insanely perky, and left for work, praying for an uneventful day. He had also said they'd be keeping him a little longer than he thought, but would let me know when he got back into town.

When I got to work, the kids were already awake and dressed, which was a pleasant surprise. They ran to me and each one grabbed a leg, so I walked into the kitchen like that, where Carl was packing his backpack. He laughed, gave me some instructions about paying preschool tuition, hugged the kids and left.

"What shall we have for breakfast today, my little aliens?"

"We not aliens!" they said happily, wanting me to do my alien voice.

"I know you are, so don't try to pretend you're not. What do people from your home planet eat for breakfast?"

They followed suit. "We eat eyeball cereal!" Cameron said.

"Yum yum. How about you, Court-On-Eee? What do you prefer?"

"I like brain pancakes," she said. They were pretty good at this. So good, in fact, that I began to wonder if they really *were* from another planet. After breakfast of cereal sans eyeballs, we flew the spaceship out the door and to my gym. Thankfully, they hadn't kicked me out. The owner had said it was the third time someone had set off the alarm accidentally, which made me feel somewhat better, but now I watched the kids every second without turning my back at all. If they ran away from me, I ran right after them, but they were always by my side. I started taking the elevator instead of having the kids climb the stairs. That way, I could distract them with having one push the button on the way up, and one push it on the way down. I guarded the alarm button in there with my life, knowing it was a big temptation to Cameron, big and red and sticking out virtually screaming, "Press me and see what happens!"

Of course being at the gym reminded Cameron that he wanted a ride in the fire engine. He asked me about 150 times if he could, both before and after my workout, both before and after Courtney stuck her hand in the elevator door. She didn't get hurt, just scared, but screamed for 15 minutes—all the way out the door and into the parking lot, and in the car, right behind my seat, straight into my ears. At least, for once, she was too distracted to fight me on getting into her seat. "Courtney, I looked at your hand and made sure. You're fine, you're just scared. It's okay, honey." I hugged her, but none of my soothing calmed her down. I was constantly amazed at how accident prone these little beings were. Combine that with being the most irrational, and it spelled trouble with a capital T. My next project could be to make personalized signs they could wear around: Danger Zone for Courtney and Fallout Zone for Cameron.

We ended up visiting the fire department, and I asked if we could sit in the fire engine. As it turns out, all the action was on the C-shift, and it was an A-shift crew on duty, so they had a fire engine sitting in the garage.

I couldn't believe this was happening—all because of Cameron's persistence. We climbed aboard. Courtney was in my lap, and Cameron climbed in on the other side, helped up by one of the firefighters that had been at the gym the day he set off the alarm. The one on my side, I recognized too, but he hadn't been there that day. "Hi, I'm Chris," he said, shaking my hand.

"My pleasure."

"Chris, what do all these buttons and switches do?" Cam asked.

"Well, these here are the emergency lights at the top. Here's the master switch that turns everything on, and the Opticom is what gives us the green lights."

"See, Cameron? If your mommy's car had one of these, it would make the red lights turn green so we could go!"

"Cool!" he said.

"We have this which controls the remote control spotlight, and side scene and rear scene flood lights. This tells us the front and rear oil pressure, fuel gauge, water and transmission temperature. This big black button is absolute shutdown. We don't ever want to have to use that." Chris's voice was really animated, and Cameron was enthralled.

"We have automatic tire chains which deploy if we're on a hill or something that's hard for the fire engine to maneuver. They also automatically retract." At this point, I started to get excited.

"Can I have that on my car?" I wondered aloud, and he laughed and continued.

"The high idle jacks up the RPM's so the alternators aren't taxed. We have auto mirrors. The blue button lets us talk to the dispatcher without engine noise. And we have radios on swivel mounts."

The kids were transfixed. They said "Wow" after everything the firefighter told us. Mentally, I was saying "Wow" as well. I loved this! I only wished Hammer was here to enjoy us enjoying it! I was keyed up to ask some questions myself, but Chris wasn't finished. He went around to the passenger side where there was a computer mounted to the dash.

"The full computer system tells all information dispatchers have about the call," he said. "It has map coordinates of where on the GPS the fire is and the nearest cross streets. It's run on a satellite system. The high school, medical facilities, and mobile home parks are fully laid out." He pressed a few buttons, with Cameron's help, and pulled up a map of the local high school. "I have more to show you in back." So we all piled out of the truck, with Chris helping Cameron jump down while still allowing Cam to feel like he was doing it all himself. They high five'd each other, and he picked Cameron up to show him the back.

"See the rear facing jumpseats?"

"Yes!" the kids said in unison.

"They have air packs in them, behind the seat." He lifted it up to demonstrate. "Here's the medical equipment," he said. "Each seat has its own air conditioning and heating unit, so everyone can control their own system."

"Sweet!" Cameron said. I was pretty sure he'd heard that from me.

"So how long do you have to get all your gear on?" I asked, trying not to drool while I pictured Hammer getting into uniform.

"From the time we get the call until the time we hear the tones, we have two minutes." Cameron and Courtney exploded with another "Wow!" and this time, I said it too. All that heavy gear must not have been easy, at least at first.

"How many firefighters are there?" I wondered.

"Well, everyone is at least an EMT. We have six paramedics, and 27 firefighters in all, nine per shift. There are A-shifts, B-shifts and C-shifts. All the action is on the C-shift, and has been that way for the last two years," he said.

"Interesting," I said, thinking about the chances of that.

"The shifts are from 7:30am-7:30am. We average about five hours of sleep a night," he said, "Sometimes less—I'm sure you know something about that, Natalie," he said, winking. I opened my mouth in surprise and amusement, and he just went right on talking. "We work 24 hours on and 48 hours off." I wasn't going to dignify his ribbing with a response.

"Any volunteers?"

"Yes, we have..." he started to count. He didn't know, so he asked another guy, who didn't know, so he went into the office and asked the boss. The boss had to check the books. This distraction thing wasn't just for kids, it seemed to do work fine on firefighters too. I'd have to remember that.

"18 certified volunteers," he said.

"Can I volunteer?" Cameron asked. Chris smiled, and told him maybe he could be the mascot for now, and in a few years could volunteer. This seemed to satisfy Cameron. He had a happy little smile on his face. I saw something in his eyes though, that turned from contentedness to mischief. He tried to mask it with an earnest expression, but his mouth curved into this funny shape it did when he was trying to get away with something or get his way. "Can we take a ride?"

You'll never believe what happened next: Just then, the alarm bell sounded, and a bunch of young, strapping guys came running out of nowhere getting things together. Must be the volunteers.

"Maybe another time, Cam!" he said, getting into his gear. "Come on!" he said to me. He walked us quickly over to a spot the kids would be safe, and the kids and I continued to watch. I knew I wouldn't get these kids out of there without a fight, so I didn't even try. Oh, who am I kidding, I wanted to watch too. This was just too cool not to watch.

"Must suddenly be a C-shift!" I said, joking. I heard Cameron repeat me, and then Courtney, which was funny. "Echo!" I said.

"Echo!"

"Echo!"

We watched everyone gear up, strap in and ride out. It was like magic. First there was nothing happening, and then suddenly it was like a bunch of bees swarming all around, and then they were gone, and the station was virtually empty again.

"Well kids, wasn't that fun!"

"Well kids, wasn't that fun!" Cameron imitated. "Yes!" Courtney said. Oh boy could I take their enthusiasm and run with it. All the better to wear you out with, my dears.

"Wonderful!"

"Wonderful!"

"Amazing!"

"Amazing!"

"Fantastic!"

"Fantastic!"

"Stupendous!"

"Stupendous!" I better quit now, I thought. Cameron was spitting all over his sister trying to say that one.

We walked back through the offices to the front door, and I thanked the woman at the front desk. She gave the kids each a piece of Halloween candy, after asking my permission, of course, and said we could come back any time. Just before we exited the building, one of the firefighters who was at the gym that fateful day in recent history cornered me. "We're all gonna miss Hammer," he said.

"I know you will," I said, smiling and looking into his eyes. He was a little older than the rest, and I wondered if he was like a father figure to Hammer.

"When you see him, tell him we're all hoping he loves his new job."

"I sure will." And on a whim, I gave this big teddy bear a hug. "I'm Natalie."

"I know. I'm Tim," he said. We said goodbye and headed for the wagon.

"Natalie, Natalie, when can we go for a ride?"

"I don't know, Cameron, but maybe if you're on extra special good boy behavior, I'll think about it, and see if Mommy and Daddy approve."

"Oh boy oh boy oh boy!" he said.

Today, they both got right into their car seats and let me strap them in without fighting me at all.

After work, I met Sam and went shopping. I was feeling refreshed because the kids had gone right down for naps, tired from the extra excitement, and satisfied with the level of it, for once.

The next day, unfortunately, I didn't have anything to match the fire department excitement with, and I had to be more imaginative than usual with my activities for these kids. I assigned Cameron with the task of protecting us from bad pirates. Courtney's job was to recharge Cameron's power, which she did by giving him a kiss on the cheek every time he was successful and a hug every other time—I was promoting sibling love, here.

"Here is your silver and gold crested sword, Sir Cameron." I knighted him, presenting the imaginary sword, and then kissed his head. We had been playing like this for two hours and it was time for lunch. Courtney had supplied plenty of hugs and kisses, so I presented her with a matching gold and silver crown. She danced around in circles, making herself dizzy and falling on her rump. Thankfully, she was in a happy mood so just laughed it off instead of crying.

"What would the knight and the fair maiden like for lunch today?" They laughed and told me they wanted a feast of epic proportions. Or, in their words: mac and cheese. They helped me make it, stirring in the butter, milk and cheese powder and adding in some real cheese to melt. It fascinated them how these things could make such a yummy lunch. I gave them some apple slices that they wanted to dip in peanut butter, so I obliged. After all, this was a feast. They even got Oreos for dessert. They had orange and black faces, so I took pictures of them for their parents in honor of Halloween, which was the next day. Their stomachs were very, very full and starting to weigh them down, so we didn't have trouble getting to sleep that day. Hallelujah.

Before their nap, we were petting Wanda, and Cameron asked me if I had a kitty. "I sure do."

"What's your kitty's name?"

"Kiki."

"Can Kiki visit us? Kiki meet Wanda?"

"We'll see, Cam." Kiki didn't like riding in cars too much. Then I had a thought. "What about you all come over to visit me and Kiki on Halloween?"

"Trick or treat at your house?"

"Yep. Sound good?"

"Sounds good!"

"Okay!" He bounced up and down on the bed and hugged me.

"If you're lucky, Hammer might be there."

"Cool!"

"Do you know what your costume is going to be?"

"No. Mommy and I go shopping tonight."

"Well, you can think about what you want to be before you go to sleep. Maybe the answer will come to you in a dream," I said, touching his forehead before I slipped out and closed the door. He was already looking through the cracks in the blinds, up at the sky for ideas.

After they woke up, we did some puzzles and coloring, and then I taught them how to do jumping jacks. They loved the jumping jacks, and I believe we did about 200 of them, so they were good and worn out when their dad got home.

That night, Hammer was waiting for me when I got to my apartment. He stood outside my door, leaning against a beam. I got out of my car and asked if everything was okay. He hugged me hard.

"You might not want to do that," I tried to warn him. "I'm sure I have food and paint all over me from the day…"

"I don't care." He kept hugging me. Finally, he released me.

I studied his face. "Hi," I said.

"Hi," he said, somewhat apologetically. "I guess I missed you."

"Let's go inside," I said, smiling. We went inside and closed the door.

"I missed you too," I said. "A lot." I took his keys and put them in his jacket pocket, took his jacket off and put it in the closet. Then, I took off his shoes and socks. And then, I removed his shirt, and then my shirt, and the rest of it, and took him by the hand. I turned on the shower, and we got in.

I shampooed his hair and rinsed it, and then did my own. I conditioned my hair (he doesn't use the stuff, being a manly man and all). I put body wash on the cool natural sponge thing, and lathered up his whole body, and then rinsed him. I started to do myself, and he took the sponge away. "Let me do it," he said shyly but firmly.

"Okay."

He took his time with everything, especially my back. He washed me from behind, using his hands, not the sponge. Then he started to kiss my back, starting at the top of my spine, going all the way down. He didn't know that having my back kissed was my favorite thing, ever.

The water started to cool off, which was refreshing for a minute, but then not. We laughed and he got out of the shower, wrapped me in one big purple towel, and then quickly dried himself off and wrapped another around his waist.

"How do you feel about chicken curry?" I asked.

"Only if it very very spicy," he said with an Indian accent that was dead on. I bowed.

"Hot and spicy coming right up!" I said, getting the ingredients together. He put his hands in prayer position and bowed back.

"Natalie, you know I got the job."

"Yes. I got your message. Congratulations!"

"Thanks. I'm so excited to start. But it won't be for another couple weeks, and it looks like there will always be gaps like that. So I'm going to be on call at the local department in between stints."

"Wow! The best of both worlds!" I hugged him.

"Yeah, I'm pretty happy actually. I was hoping you would be too. You know I can't—"

"Sit still. I know. And of course I'm thrilled. I want nothing less than what makes you 100% happy."

"I'm glad to hear that." His eyes twinkled.

"What's that look in your eyes?" I asked.

"What look?" he said, looking even more mysterious.

"Only that shine in your eyes, brighter than the brightest stars in the sky."

"Well, I guess I'm just happy to be back with you."

"You're so sweet. But please stop being sweet for a few, I have to cook," I said. He proceeded to help me with everything. He was so handy to have around, even in the kitchen. It secretly thrilled me to be cooking with him, but I didn't let on.

When dinner was ready, we sat down on the couch with our plates, and I got the remote and turned on some music.

"Tim will be thrilled to have you back once in a while, too, I'm sure."

"You spoke to him?"

"Yes. He said he and the guys would miss you a lot."

Hammer smiled and looked down, eyelashes hiding his expression.

I got the impression he didn't want to talk about it and get emotional, so I changed the subject. "Hey, guess what! Halloween is tomorrow."

"That's right! With all that's happened lately I completely forgot."

"Uh oh...but I bet you can think of a costume last minute, right?"

"Why, do we have plans?" he laughed.

"Well, I was going to invite you over here to give candy out to the kids with me."

"Do you have a costume?"

"Yep."

"Gonna tell me what it is?"

"Nope."

"Are Cameron and Courtney coming by?"

"Yep."

"Cool. I'm sure I can make it."

"Yeah? How sure?" I asked.

"How sure?" he repeated.

"How sure?" I said again, laughing.

"You really want to know?"

"I really want to know."

"About...this sure." And he gave me a kiss that completely floored me.

"I like it when you're this sure."

"Hmmm, me too," he said into my neck. "How sure are you that I'm going to find a costume at the last minute?"

"I'm pretty sure."

"But how sure, pretty?"

"You think you can handle knowing how sure?"

"Try me."

I decided it was time—before we got too comfortable in the routine. It was now or never, Natalie. I did a crescent kick and ended with that leg resting on his right shoulder, and then grabbed his left hand, hoisted my left leg up onto his left shoulder, and me right into his lap. "About that sure."

"Whoa. What in the world was that?"

"That was a combination kick. It's something I've been working on lately."

"Really? Where?"

"At martial arts school." I still couldn't give away the location, especially to someone who belonged to my gym.

"I had no idea."

I let it sink in, and waited. I was nervous, because everything was pretty darn perfect between us right now and I didn't want to mess it up. I wasn't sure he'd be okay with me practicing martial arts.

"So how long have you been taking it?" he asked.

"Only two years."

"Wow. So you're pretty good then."

"I have a lot yet to learn. My teacher has done it all his life."

"He?"

"Yes, he."

"How old is he?"

"I don't know, 45 to 50 I suppose."

"Married?"

"Yes."

"With kids?"

"Two."

"Are you attracted to him?"

"No. It's not like that. I take it because I want to be able to defend myself or my loved ones if I ever need to."

"I understand that."

"Do you? I'm glad. Because in my life, I've been messed with a lot."

"By whom?"

"By men who think that just because a girl is walking on the sidewalk, they have some right to her person."

"I see."

"Are you going to be okay with this?"

He just looked at me for a minute. "Natalie, I'm surprised at you."

Oh jeez. Here we go. "Why?"

"Well, that you haven't told me about it, for one."

"I was just waiting for the right moment. It didn't come until tonight. I'm sorry." I waited for the explosion, for him to get huffy, for whatever it was that he was surprised and upset about.

"That's okay. But I'm also surprised that you would think I wouldn't be okay with this."

"Really?"

"Yes. I mean, you can do whatever you want, and the fact that you're a secret rebel just makes me like you even more. I knew there was something about you I couldn't figure out. Now I know what it is. That explains the leather you wore the day you drove us to the lake. At least I think it does."

I swallowed. "It does." He didn't have to know that the leather was strategically placed solely to catch his eye.

"Natalie, I'm a 21st century guy. Liberal. I want you to be happy, and if doing martial arts makes you happy, hey. Plus I just find you endlessly interesting…everything about you, from how you decorate to what you do in your spare time."

I put my finger on his lips, silencing him. "I guess I'm not used to 21st century guys."

"Well, get used to us. We do exist. And while you're at it, show me some more moves."

I hugged him. "I love you," I said. "Um. I mean…"

He laughed. "I know what you meant. You were relieved I wasn't upset. It's cool." I hugged him again, and then I kissed him. And then I showed him some more moves—in the boudoir.

A Truly Haunting Halloween

I went to the store in the morning to get some candy. Somehow, all of mine had disappeared. I had no idea how that had happened. I was innocent. I blamed Kiki. After all, she was there all day while I was at work. I had a cat with a sweet tooth.

You'll never guess who I ran into at the store.

"Hey," I said.

"Oh my god! Are you stalking me?" Sam asked, laughing.

"I admit it. I have nothing better to do than stalk you. I stalked you even before we met, and implanted a chip in your brain to make you make oogly-googly faces at the baby in my arms that day."

She laughed. "You getting candy for the trick-or-treaters?"

"Yep. Hammer is coming over and the kids I nanny for are going to stop by, along with the rest of the neighborhood. Hopefully. I've got a ton of candy here. How about you? Buying candy for the bank or for home?"

"Bank. Kids don't really come to my neighborhood. Too ghetto I guess."

"Why don't you come over? We'll both be dressed up."

"In that case, I wouldn't miss it. What's Hammer going to be?"

"No idea. I wouldn't tell him, so he wouldn't tell me."

"Not doing the couple costume thing yet, hmm?"

"Plenty of time for that. A little mystery is a good thing."

She smiled. "What time should I come over?"

"Anytime after 6 works. Candy store doors close at 10pm."

"Cool. I'll probably show up with a couple kids I rented for the evening," she said. She babysat her niece and nephew occasionally.

"In costume?"

"Them-yes. Me-maybe."

"Maybe is better than no. See you tonight."

"See you then."

Things were shaping up nicely for Halloween. It was my favorite holiday, so as long as everything went well, then Thanksgiving and Christmas would be a breeze.

The first knock on the door came at 5:35pm. It was Hammer. When I saw him, I let out a shriek of delight. It couldn't be helped. He was Willy Wonka—perfect.

"I was expecting you to be a firefighter!"

"I figured you were. I'm not that predictable, baby."

"I love it when you surprise me."

He smiled and surveyed me. "Likewise. I expected a martial artist."

I was dressed as a geisha. I wanted to keep with the theme, but show him my feminine side too. It might make for some fun later, especially when he saw what was underneath.

Kiki came running out of the bathroom to greet him. She was dressed in leather. Hammer laughed like I'd never seen him laugh before.

"It took her a while to get ready, so be sure to pay compliments," I whispered. Kiki sported a leather vest with stretchy string in back, a leather hat, and matching miniskirt. I had even painted her nails—front paws red, back paws black. She chose that over the mini biker booties I'd almost gotten. She sidled up to Hammer, strutting her stuff.

"Everything about you is sexy. Even your cat." he said, grinning. "Nice outfit, Kiki. Now she just needs a man to flaunt it for."

As if right on cue, the doorbell rang. Wanda came running in first, dressed as a 70's disco cat with a tiny fro wig on his head that would've looked natural because he was so fluffy, except that it was rainbow colored. He ignored everyone and ran straight to the food bowl in the kitchen. After eating like he'd been fasting for months, he went up and greeted Kiki, sniffing everything from her nose all the way to her derriere. Apparently it all met with his approval, because he laid down and bared his belly in a sign of submission.

Cameron and Courtney stood at the door. "Trick or treat!" they shouted, their parents smiling behind them.

"Well hello," I said, bowing and giving them hugs.

"Looks like we have Woodstock and Tweety Bird here tonight!" They looked adorable—all that showed were their little faces. The rest of them were zipped into costumes.

I threw a handful of candy into both pumpkins, followed by a mini vacation toothbrush and toothpaste kit. Camalia and Carl asked if they could have a word with me, so Hammer watched the kids while we stepped outside into the crisp autumn night.

"Natalie, we were thinking, if you're going to be here the rest of the night handing out candy…"

"I am."

"We would love for you to watch the kids while we snuck out and saw a movie. If not, it's okay, but we never get to do things alone as you know, and are sure the kids would love to hang out with you while you greet other little goblins."

"Say no more. I'd be more than happy to do it."

"Oh Natalie, thank you. We'll pay you extra for this."

"That's not necessary, but thanks. What time do you think you'll be back? I would offer to let them spend the night, but I don't really have room."

"Understood. It shouldn't be long after 11pm."

"Works for me."

They snuck away, and the kids were too distracted by Sam showing up a few minutes later with her charges, Shrek & Shrek II, to notice. Sam had tried to get the little girl to dress as the princess, but she wanted to be green, so we had identical trolls. Introductions were made, and the four kids were fast friends. They took charge of answering the door, and Sam and I made sure they were only giving each goblin one kid handful of candy. Hammer made himself busy eliminating surplus stash. There were pirates, ghosts, vampires, princesses, sorcerers, Muppets, Nemo, and even the Fruit of the Loom crew showed up. One family dressed as Hostess products—a Twinkie, a Ding Dong, a Hoho, and a Suzy Q. They got my vote for most original.

Soon, diapers needed changing, so Hammer took my place as Overseer of Operations, while I attended to the Proper Disposal of Poop.

At 9:25, the slew of kids coming to the door had finally slowed. I didn't think there would be much more than a couple stragglers, so I suggested putting in a movie. The kids all gave a big "Hoorah!" at that idea, so I put the bowl of remaining candy outside and we all settled into the couch. We were about 10 minutes into Shrek II, which Sam had brought over in honor of her two little trolls, when Hammer's pager went off.

We looked at each other. "Babe, I gotta go," he said.

"I know. I knew something would have to happen tonight or it just wouldn't be a real Halloween."

Cameron was watching with rapt attention. "Babe, can I go too?" he asked.

"That's Ms. Natalie to you, and no Cameron, you can't. Your parents are coming back to get you in a couple hours."

"Okay," he said, lower lip jutting out in true pouting fashion.

Hammer kissed me and was out the door. I sighed. Courtney sighed. Cameron sighed. Shrek I and Shrek II sighed. Sam giggled.

And then Hammer came back. "That was quick," I noted.

"My car won't start. Can I borrow yours?"

"Sure." I found my keys and tossed them to him. "Be safe," I said, blowing him an air kiss.

"Thanks," he said, giving me a little smile. "I'll be back as soon as I can!" and he was gone.

And then he was back, out of breath. "Okay, your car has a flat."

"What?"

"Right rear."

"Fudge."

"Fudge! Fudge! Fudge! Can I have some fudge?" sang the kid choir. "Flat tire fudge! Flat tire fudge! Mmmmmmm!"

"Everybody settle down. Shhhhhhh." I heard four shhhhhh's and some giggling, and it was quiet.

"He could use mine, but I wouldn't trust it," Sam said. It had been breaking down quite a lot in the past weeks and months—which was one reason why we didn't take it to California.

"Damn, where's the Spyder when we really need it?" I said without thinking.

"Damn!" Cameron said. I cringed and decided to let it slide, hoping that not making a big deal out of it would work and he would forget it. Sam laughed silently. Hammer just stood there wondering what to do.

"I'll have the guys come and get me. They're really short staffed tonight," he said.

"Okay, good idea," I said, trying to be encouraging. "By the way, what caught fire?"

"I'm not sure, I'll ask when I call in." He stepped outside. We all looked at each other and waited, Shrek singing in the background. He came back in, and I met him at the door in hopes that the kids wouldn't hear us. "An office building next to the movie theater."

"Which movie theater?"

"The one downtown."

"*Oh no.*" The theater was in an old-fashioned building attached to some offices and restaurants. It was a cute complex, and the one Courtney and Cameron's parents had gone to.

Minutes later, the fire engine pulled up to my apartment building. Thankfully, they hadn't flipped the siren switch yet. There was only one person in it, driving. He got out and threw Hammer his fire suit. Hammer did an expert job of getting his gear on in less than two minutes. I timed it. "Nice work!" I said. He smiled, got in, and took off.

I shook my head and thought about what a crazy night this had turned into. As we all filed back into the apartment, I noticed someone was missing. "Where's Cameron?" Nobody had an answer. "Oh my God," I said with a feeling of dread in the pit of my stomach. I opened the door and ran alongside my apartment complex, yelling at the fire engine to stop. Everyone ran after me. I had Tweety Bird, Shrek I, Shrek II, and a magician following me, the geisha, Kinky Kiki and Wacky Wanda taking up the slack, all of us in hot pursuit of Willy Wonka and Woodstock.

By this time, we were a good half mile from my apartment. Luckily, I didn't have to do my disappearing act in front of everyone to reappear where the firefighters could see me, because the brake lights came on. Either they'd seen me, or they'd discovered Cameron, or both. The engine started to reverse, and we ran up to it.

"We don't have time to take you back. Just get in!" Hammer instructed. I didn't ask questions. I just climbed aboard, as best I could in my Geisha getup, carrying a couple characters, followed by the rest of the costumed clan. Cameron was thrilled to see me, even though I had given him my best death glare. He stood up, hugged my leg and thanked me for finally letting him go for a ride in a fire engine.

"This isn't how I imagined our first ride to go, Cameron," I said, sitting him back down, "but I had no choice since you snuck into the truck. Your parents are sure going to hear about this," I said, hoping to put the fear of God, Allah, and whoever else into him, and hoping the C's were okay. Cameron looked worried about the possibility of a punishment for a second, and then got distracted by the sound of the sirens. I looked back, and Kiki and Wanda were on the sidewalk. At least one of them had had the presence of mind to stop before getting to the road. I imagined it was probably Kiki, because I didn't have much faith in boy Wanda.

We sped to the scene. Cameron and Courtney were in my lap, and Sam's niece and nephew in hers. I called to see if the C's had maybe changed their minds and decided to do something else, but when I got the voicemail on the cell and at home, I figured they had stuck with the original plan.

As we pulled up, I saw that the blaze was bigger than I'd imagined. The office building was burned to the ground, and over half the movie theater was also engulfed. There were a smaller fire truck, two ambulances, a medic and three cop cars. The smaller truck had tried with limited supplies to douse the fire, to no avail. Several moviegoers stood outside, wrapped in blankets, watching the blaze—escapees. Hammer helped us all out of the truck and out of the way, and we stood back while they undid the hoses and everything. Cameron was spellbound, watching the firefighters, and I could see his little brain memorizing where all the gear was. I had to fight to keep him from running over and getting in the way. Sam struggled with the trolls, too. I thought how convenient it'd be to cordon them off so they wouldn't go anywhere. Those kid leashes would've come in handy right about now...

Hammer and his partner got the fire down a little bit, but one of them had to go in to see if anyone was stuck inside the theater. I didn't know which, but I was praying to the aforementioned deities that it wouldn't be Hammer. Unfortunately there were 6 cinemas, and they hadn't told me which movie they were seeing, so I had no way of knowing where they were, only that they'd gone to this theater. I was so glad I hadn't told the kids where their parents had gone—just in case.

"Sam, can you handle them for a few minutes while I go check and see if I can find their parents?" I whispered.

"You got it, girl," she said. Her eyes were glassy, but I knew she was in control.

I made my way over to the folks standing there, wrapped in blankets. There were so many of them, and it was easy to see their faces because the fire was burning brightly, even though they stood far from it. I walked around the group, and unfortunately, the two faces I wanted to see were the two faces I didn't. I jogged back to Sam and the kids, and shook my head. She looked down and closed her eyes. The kids were busy watching the fire and didn't pay much attention to our facial expressions.

Suddenly, the doors burst open. The older firefighter I had met at the station came through, carrying someone. It looked like the body of a small child. Hammer turned and looked at me, blew me an air kiss, which I caught after he ran inside. It was his turn to search for survivors, or victims. I started crying. I couldn't help it. I tried to keep the tears silent, so the kids wouldn't catch on, but Cameron noticed and asked me what was wrong.

"Cameron, it's the smoke from when I went closer, that's all," I said. He hugged my leg anyway.

"You be okay, Natalie." I picked him up and hugged his little body.

We waited and Hammer came out three minutes later with another body, this time an adult. But it wasn't either of the C's. The tears were rolling down my face now. I didn't realize it'd be so hard to watch my boyfriend do his job, but it was harder than anything I'd ever done, harder than any martial arts move. He signaled to the other guys that the building was clear of survivors, and they went to town on extinguishing the flames. He came over and told me privately that there were bodies in the theater, but burned beyond recognition. As I hugged him, I felt my throat close up, and held back the hot tears that were pushing to get out. I knew something wasn't right. Luckily, he didn't have much time to comfort me, so I could escape unnoticed one more time. I told Sam there was something I had to do, quickly helped her load the kids into the fire engine, and told them to wait for me, that I'd be back in five.

I knew I needed to check things out inside. I knew now that I could disappear and reappear somewhere else, but didn't know if I was impenetrable to fire. This was a life and death situation, however; no time to hem and haw over what-if scenarios. I could always teleport myself right on out of there if I started to feel the burn.

I closed my eyes, focused, and entered the theater, quickly lowering myself all the way down to the ground to avoid smoke as much as possible. Oddly, I could still breathe even with the smoke in the air, and when I opened my eyes, could see quite clearly. It was like I was wearing night vision goggles.

The lobby was clear of people. I checked the bathrooms—also clear. Now I'd attend to the task of the six theaters.

They were quite large, but I found I could mentally map each room instantly, and sort of GPS it for signs of life. Methodically, I visited each theater and scanned it in about 30 seconds. No blips on the radar; not a one. The firefighters were extremely thorough. The C's were not inside. They hadn't been among the bodies extricated from the building, either. A gi-normous wave of relief washed over me.

I closed my eyes, and scanned the parking lot in my mind. Seeing that there was no one loitering behind the fire engine, I reappeared there, taking a long, deep, cleansing breath. These had been the longest five minutes of my life.

Knowing Hammer was fine and had already left, I walked around to Sam and the kids. Sam looked worried, but smiled when she saw me, whispering to me that she'd called a cab. All the kids were asleep, except of course Cameron, still wide-eyed. He asked me if I'd gone to the bathroom, and I said yes, smiling inside at his never-ending curiosity and concern.

The cab pulled up, perfectly timed, and we transferred the sleeping kidlets into it. The firefighter, whose name I didn't know, drove away in the engine.

On the taxi ride back, I was finally able to calm down somewhat. It was getting really late, and I needed to make sure the cats were okay, make sure no one had broken into my apartment, and get the kids to bed.

When we got to my apartment, Sam gave me a hug, took the groggy trolls by the hands, and left. I went inside with my two little yellow birds and closed the door. Kiki and Wanda were curled up together on the easy chair. I turned the TV on, and Cameron watched, hypnotized. I scooped up Courtney, and dialed the parents' home number. Still no response.

A few minutes later, I saw headlights in front of my apartment, so I peeked through the curtains. The C's got out. How did they look? Guilty.

They came to the door, and I answered it. Cam ran and greeted them with warm hugs. The first words out of Cameron's mouth spilled it about the fire engine ride, and the fire.

"Wow, Natalie, you've had quite a night!" they said. I know they were hoping I'd forget that they were two hours late, but I didn't. They saw the question marks in my eyes. They saw that my eyes were red from smoke and crying, and I could tell that they felt even more guilt. I didn't want them to feel that, but in truth, it'd been a long, traumatic night for my crew and I, so they probably deserved it.

"Sorry you couldn't reach us. We went to dinner and then decided to rent a movie instead of sitting in a dark theater with a bunch of strangers seeing something we didn't really care to see. We turned off the phones."

"I see. Well, it's okay, I was just really worried because the theater you were supposedly in burned down tonight. Hammer got the call, his car wouldn't start, and mine had a flat, so the fire engine had to come and pick him up. Cameron snuck into it when the guys were getting their gear on. It was pandemonium. I figured it out quickly, but the truck was a few blocks away from my apartment by then, and I wasn't sure when they would discover him. So I took off running, and everyone followed me. By that time, it was too late to go back, so we were along for the ride." I paused, letting this information sink in. "I'm just glad you're okay," I finished.

"So that's how it went. Well Cameron, we will have to talk about this," his mother said, giving him the evil eye, and asked him to get Wanda. Courtney was already asleep, so her father picked her up, and they headed out. "See you Monday," they said. We were all exhausted, so we didn't prolong the goodbyes.

I closed the door and took a deep breath. It felt oddly good to finally rat Cameron out for once, for something that he'd done that caused havoc.

I hoped Hammer would come to my apartment instead of going home, but I wasn't sure. I left him a note outside the door, just in case, to call my cell phone and wake me up to open the door. Then I crashed.

I've heard we dream every night, even if we don't remember them sometimes. That night, I didn't remember mine and I was glad. What I did remember was Hammer calling in the middle of the night, hearing his voice and feeling blissful to have his warm body beside me. He did this thing in the middle of the night where he would pull me very close and spoon, burrowing his face into my hair. It happened every time I fidgeted and I don't think he even realized he did it, it was just a natural protective gesture. The urge to shield from harm was in his blood and I loved it. I loved him. I wanted to tell him, but again I was waiting for the right moment.

We spent Sunday cleaning up the aftermath of the holiday, and when we finished, he took me out to an early dinner. We got back, and Kiki had words for me. I'd forgotten to undo her costume, and she was miffed. After I apologized and gave her some affection, Hammer and I went to bed. I felt so wonderful in his arms. He made me feel gorgeous, even when I didn't wear makeup. That level of comfort, excitement, and trust, was hard earned in my life, and I didn't take one second of it for granted.

Unfortunately, Monday came all too soon.

The kids were boisterous as usual, challenging my choices for clothes. I had abandoned the rule of two and didn't let them choose what to wear anymore. I crept into their rooms before they woke up and chose an outfit. They were still rebelling against this, asking me to open the drawer and find another shirt or pair of pants. I gave it another week before they stopped wasting their energy on that. For now, I had to distract them with thoughts of breakfast.

This week, Cameron again asked "Why" to everything. Why I cut sandwiches diagonally, why did they have a girl nanny instead of a boy nanny, why did I wear makeup, why did I have a boyfriend, why did they have to brush their teeth, why did the neighbor's dog always bark when we came home? Why? Why why *why*?

I think I was about to go crazy with the whys, since today was a no-preschool day. Then I figured out what I wanted to do. I wanted to see the Lollipop Man. Because he was part of the Lollipop Guild, and he would make everything all better in just a couple licks—of a lollipop, I mean, not the kind of licks that the kids probably deserved. I was kind of glad Cameron was with us today, because when I took Courtney alone, she asked me repeatedly, "Is that your coffee?" until I answered her. It sounded more like "Dat your coffee?" If I didn't answer, she would ask again and again. If I did answer, she would ask again and again. I tried thinking of things to distract her with, but my brain usually wasn't awake enough to be brilliant, especially when I had just started sipping my coffee.

We pulled up and the barista gave me a knowing look. "Rough morning?"

"You might say that. How about you?"

"Fine and dandy, miss. Every day is a new beginning." I wished I could be that upbeat and optimistic. "What'll it be?"

"One Tequila Sunrise and two lollipops, please." He laughed and handed over the lollipops. I unwrapped them and handed them back to the kids. "Make that one coconut mocha and one biscotti for me. Thanks." If I couldn't have a tropical alcoholic drink, I could sure have a tropical coffee drink.

He asked me how I was doing. I said fine. He called my bluff.

"Are you really okay?"

"Why, whatever do you mean?" I asked, still feigning innocence.

"I heard about the shenanigans at the gym across the street," he said. I laughed.

"You did, huh? News travels fast. That grapevine just keeps on growing."

"So it isn't true?"

"Depends. What'd you hear?" I flashed my finger to tell him to hold on a sec, turned up the radio, and moved the balance to the back speakers so the kids couldn't listen, and closed the back windows. They were too busy with their lollipops to pay attention, but I did wish I had a partition between the front and back seats just for such occasions.

"That this little man pulled the fire alarm and caused quite a stir."

"Well, that part is true. Anything else?"

"That you all got to ride in a fire engine the other night."

"Well, now I don't have any news to tell you." Bummer. I like surprising people with the latest. "How is a girl supposed to surprise her favorite barista if the grapevine gets there before she does?"

"That grapevine gets here early and likes his coffee strong."

"Hmm. Who told you about all this? You must have an inside connection, because the fire engine ride only happened two nights ago."

"A journalist, or a barista, can never reveal his source."

"Oh, come on. You have more dirt on me than I have on you. Who's the leak?"

"Here." He handed me the local paper, grinning like a Cheshire cat.

"Is this what you meant by a journalist…?" What I was about to say faded as I looked in astonishment at the faces staring out at me.

There, on the front page of the local paper, was a 3-photo spread of the fire. That much was to be expected—it'd been a huge fire, and the movie theater was a popular place. Having no movies for the holidays, in our town, was a big deal. Underneath that, though, there was a blurb about some trick-or-treaters being caught up in the commotion. This included two photos: one of us in the fire engine and one of all of us getting out of the engine in our costumes. As luck would have it, my face was in the middle of the shot—the focal point. Cameron and Courtney were right in front of me. I had just helped them out of the engine, and it looked like I had totally lost control because they were both in motion, trying to run away. Seconds later, I had caught them both but of course, the photo didn't capture that. Sam and her kids were behind us, but you could only see from the waist down on Sam, and the Shrek costumes covered the faces of her niece and nephew. Now I was the one asking why. Why why *why* did it have to be like that? Why couldn't the person have taken a picture of Sam and the trolls instead? Or if they did, why couldn't the newspaper have run that one? Why weren't the photos of just the fire?

I gawked at the spread. I knew I was ruined. My reputation as a nanny in Washington State was tarnished. I may even have to leave the country, I thought. I knew my previous family missed me, but wondered if they missed me enough to consider taking me back.

The barista saw the look on my face, and realized I wasn't having a cute, fun reaction to what was supposed to be a cute, fun couple of photos. "Sorry," he said. "I thought you'd think it was amusing."

"Well, I would, but I try to keep a low profile," I said.

I could see the wheels spinning in his head, thinking of something to say that could make me feel better. "It's only the local paper," he said. That didn't really do it. My stomach felt like someone was twisting it into a taffy spiral. Maybe I would save the coconut mocha for later. Yes, definitely a good idea.

"Well, I'm sure the parents will laugh in about 10 years when they find it in the 'Toddler Years' scrapbook," I said, thanking him, and drove away.

Then I drove back through. "One more thing," I said. "Who told you about the fake fire at the gym?"

"If I tell you, you promise not to give me away, right?"

"Hey, at least one of us deserves not to have their personal and professional life on the front page."

"How is it personal?" he asked. "It's just your job, right?"

"Keep my secret if I keep yours?" I asked.

"Deal," he said, sticking out his hand. I shook it.

"I'm dating a firefighter."

"Serious? Which one?"

"Hammer."

"Oh my God, I know Hammer! He stops in once in a while with the guys."

"So... was he the one who told you?"

"Nope. It was Tim, the older guy."

I breathed a sigh of relief. Not that I thought my own boyfriend was spreading stories, but I was glad anyway. "I know Tim. He's a good guy," I said.

"Yeah, he is. We are actually the same age. We went to school together," he said.

"Cool. It is a small world," I said.

"Well, it's a small town anyway."

"Yeah." This reminded me of just how small it was and how gossip spread like wildfire. Pun intended. I guess I looked concerned again, because he reminded me that 100 years from now, none of this would matter. I laughed, wanting him to think it worked, said goodbye, and drove away.

We went to the park, and Cameron wanted to go down the highest slides, but the little daredevil was still small enough that he could easily hurt himself, so I told him to stick to the smaller ones, and my eyes were constantly on him. I let him run around while I pushed Courtney, because all she ever wanted to do at the park was swing. While pushing and watching, my little wheels were spinning.

Had this been a prank that the firefighters played on me? I could see them getting that newspaper printed. And the gym, coffee stand and fire station were all in the same 2-block radius, so it wasn't like they couldn't see me stop there for coffee occasionally. After an hour of pushing and watching and thinking, I pried Courtney out of the child swing, kicking and screaming, and told them we were going to the store.

This usually worked to get them to behave. The store meant food, treats, and sometimes looking at the crabs in the tank, all piled on each other. If I were those crabs, I'd lobby for better pre-death-sentence conditions. I would pinch anyone who tried to crowd me in like that, but maybe they didn't have space issues. Maybe they were bubble-free and perfectly happy to be there. Maybe they knew they could be like the Cuban crabs, being crunched by a car on the way to or from the sea, and preferred the safer conditions the U.S. offered. Maybe they were peaceful, non-resistant crabs who had studied the ways of Zen.

I came out of my reverie in front of the crab case. Cameron and Courtney were enthralled. I was glad, because I didn't want to take them to the zoo until they were a little older. Courtney's legs tired out too quickly, and I could push the stroller for miles, but she would only sit in it for 20 minutes before wanting to walk. The aquarium was a better plan, because it was much smaller. It was always so crowded though, and I would take no chances with these two. I had already seen what they could do in a small town. If let loose in the big city, who knows what mayhem they might muster up. The C's had encouraged me to do these grand adventure days, but so far, I had stuck to the local scene, and, especially after recent events, thought it best to keep it that way.

With these thoughts rolling around in my head, I made my way to the store exit, a kid holding each hand. I dreaded this moment, but bit the bullet and grabbed a newspaper from the machine. I rolled it up quickly, not looking at it yet.

We got to the parking lot, got in the car safely and buckled up. I opened the paper, and there we were. No joke, no prank, just good down home reporting. Who had taken this photo? I didn't remember a flash going off. But then again, I had been a little distracted, and there was a fire so I probably wouldn't have noticed anyway. I scanned the page. The word "Anonymous" was typed in tiny letters under each photo, and that was it. Well, if Anonymous was a last name, it wouldn't be common. It would be Greek, probably. So I would find Mr. or Ms. Anonymous in the phone book, call them up, and give them a ration about respecting people's privacy.

I started thinking though, what if I called the newspaper and asked them. Weren't they supposed to ask permission to use my image? Even if the image was just my face in a geisha outfit? Blast the paparazzi. If I'd gone to Lake Como to be with George Clooney, it would be a lot worse. At least there was that. And at least there were no captions under the photos. "Naughty Natalie—Not in Control?" for the one, and "Costumed Clan to the Rescue!" for the other. Maybe I should take pictures and write for the paper since I'd be needing a new career anyway after the tarnishing of my reputation.

A knock on my window startled me. It was a smiling elderly woman. I checked and made sure I wasn't in the handicapped spot, and rolled down the window. "Yes?"

"Excuse me, dear, is this you?" she showed me the photo.

Well, I could've been dishonest and told her no, claiming she had poor eyesight. But I decided to be respectful and come clean. "Yes, ma'am."

She said, with a twinkle in her eye, "Can I have your autograph?"

I giggled. "Sure," I said. I was so traumatized, but this whole thing was out of control and I didn't know what else to do at this point. She thanked me and walked away, and I laughed until tears came out my eyes. I was laughing and crying, again, in the parking lot.

"What's an ottografffff?" Cameron asked. "That like guhrafff? Can I have a guhrafff?" Cameron asked.

"Is giraffe your favorite animal?"

"Yep. guhrafff my favorite."

"What's yours, Court?"

"Horsies! I love horsies!"

So now I knew what to get them for Christmas. I was emotionally and physically exhausted after just the morning. So I headed home and made the kids some lunch. They fought over which plates they got again. That was Cameron's thing—he always wanted whatever Courtney got.

I thought how great buying just two of each plate in the first place would've been, so we didn't have this issue—epically great.

Right after lunch, Courtney said she had to go poopy. I didn't know whether to believe her, because I had been trying to potty train her but most of the time when Cameron said he needed to go poopy, Courtney said the same thing shortly thereafter. I decided to humor her, so she sat on the toilet and nothing came out. I showed her the toilet paper with nothing on it, and she said "Oh well."

"So it's nap time, kidlets," I said.

"No, no, no!" Cameron said, running upstairs. You'd think he'd want to run away from the general vicinity of his bedroom, but he didn't. He ran straight toward it.

"How about this," I bargained. "I'll read you two stories after you wake up if you go straight to sleep today. I saw them considering it. "You can be together for both stories." They looked at each other. "Deal?"

"Deal!" they said at the same time.

I put them down for nap, and put myself down directly as well.

I woke up an hour later, feeling refreshed and somewhat better about life. Maybe the parents wouldn't see the newspaper, I thought. That fantasy lasted about two seconds, until I remembered the tight-knit community of parents and how everyone knew everyone else's business. It seemed people were getting close to knowing mine as it happened. I just hoped they wouldn't pass me up and start knowing beforehand, because if they did it'd be hard to keep up with my life.

This community of parents, though, they all felt the need to inform each other about the tiniest things. I figured it was only a matter of time—maybe two days, tops.

I woke the kids up, and Cameron insisted on holding onto my leg as I woke up Courtney. I had her in my arms when Cameron decided he wanted to sit down and have me drag him. This wasn't going to happen, so I put Courtney down for a minute, and pried Cameron off my leg. He suctioned right back on like an octopus, his arms and legs like tentacles wrapped around me. We went through this a couple more times until I threatened no story instead of two, and he let go. I heard a giggle from the next room, which happened to be their parents' room, so I high tailed it in there.

In the time it'd taken me to get the giant squid off my leg, Courtney had taken off her clothes, and her diaper.

She'd had diarrhea during her nap, and was dancing around in a little circle, singing, "I have poopy on my bottom!"

"She have poopy on her bottom!" Cameron repeated, delighted.

"Courtney, stop moving right now," I said, calmly but firmly.

"No! I have poopy on my bottom!" Cameron followed her, pointing and repeating her little song. I chased, but didn't catch the poopy monster.

"You got poopy on the carpet!" I said. Courtney just laughed and danced in the mess she'd made. Every time I went near her, she ran away, just out of reach. Cameron also seemed ecstatic at the mess. "Cameron! Please go get me the baby wipes!" I said.

"Okay," he said, happier still to be put in charge of something. He came back and handed me the plastic container. I asked him to get a towel from the bathroom and put it on the couch. I wasn't going to take Courtney downstairs dripping dung. I was fuming again, but trying to stay with it this time and not go into my inner dojo happy place.

I finally caught her, and Cameron had followed instructions so I laid her carefully on the towel, and then asked Cameron to go and get a diaper from his room, where they were kept. He came back with a Pull-up instead. I thanked him and asked him if that was really a diaper. "Oh," he said, smacking his forehead as if to say duh, and came back with a diaper a minute later.

"Thanks, Cameron!"

"You're welcome!" I got the diaper changed, with Cameron trying to stick his little fingers in the fasteners to help me and getting in the way. I'd had just about enough of their antics for the day. It took a lot to praise Cameron. I just wanted to go to the gym and work out for hours. I sat them down and talked to them, and told them we wouldn't have story time today or go outside to play.

"Have you been on good behavior?" I asked.

They thought about it. "No," Cameron said.

"What did you do that was bad behavior?"

"I don't know," Cam said.

"Courtney?" She tried to hide her face in her hands and look cute, but Cameron and I weren't buying the cuteness routine.

"Did you take off your diaper?"

"Yes."

"Who takes off your diaper?"

"You do."

"Who's in charge?"

"I am!" Cameron said.

"No you're not. *You* are three years old. Who's in charge?"

"Natalie in charge!" he said.

"That's right!"

"Who's in charge of dealing with diapers?"

"Natalie!"

"That's right. Where does Natalie take off diapers?"

"On the changing table," Cameron said.

"Very good, Cameron. Courtney, I'm going to tell your parents that you were on bad behavior today. I have to explain why there is still poopy on the carpet. Poopy is not easy to get out of the carpet," I said.

"Sorry," Courtney said.

"It's okay. Next time you have a poopy diaper, what will you do?"

"I tell Natalie."

"Yes, you tell Natalie. Who takes off your diaper, and who's in charge?"

"Natalie," they said in unison, with good eye contact and no sideways glances or giggling. Satisfied that they'd gotten the lesson, I continued. "Now we're going to watch a movie, and I want you to sit still the whole time. We stay inside today. Bad behavior means no playing outside." And bad behavior makes Natalie very cranky, I thought.

I put in a movie, and made little bags of popcorn. They didn't even touch it. What kids don't like popcorn? I was beginning to think they truly were aliens and I hoped I hadn't offended anyone on the home planet. Maybe popcorn was thought to be sacred there. All hail tiny kernels of corn, miracle of stovetop and microwave, with Orville Redenbacher as the leader...

I drew a bath the minute I got home, not bothering to get the mail or check messages. When the water was almost cold, I got out, fell into bed, and didn't wake up for a good two hours.

Walking back from getting the mail, I noticed the button on my answering machine flashing. It was Sam, asking me if I'd like to grab dinner tonight. That was just what I needed, so I accepted and we met at our usual spot.

Her eyes were red. "Ruh roh," I said. "What happened?"

"Mm...mm...Marty..." and she started crying again. This was the first time I'd ever seen her cry. I moved over next to her and put my arm around her. She didn't have a dainty feminine cry, like the ladies in black and white movies that had to borrow a handkerchief from the handsome man at the next table. I was glad. I didn't think I could respect a girl who cried like that. Kind of like when a girl shakes your hand and it's limp, no grip. I hate that too. You just know the girl is going to be fake, through and through, just because of her fake handshake. Anyway, I'm sure Sam didn't have that kind of handshake, and now she was crying silently, really hard.

"*What?* Did you break up?" They'd been doing the long distance thing for a while now, so I figured that might already be taking its toll.

"No," she said. It was all she could do to get a word out.

"Did he hurt you?"

"No," she said. I waited. Finally, it came out. "He told me he loves me," she said. And she started crying even harder than before.

"Get it all out, girl, and then we'll talk," I said, just sheltering her while she shook. Sam cried silently like this for a couple more minutes, and started breathing deeply. I started breathing deeply with her. "That's good. In, out. In, out. Up, down, Daniel-san." Finally, I got a giggle out of her. "Okay. Can you speak now?"

"One sec." She wiped her tears and blew her nose.

"In what way is Marty telling you he loves you a bad thing? Do you not love him back? Explain please."

She paused. "That's just it. I do love him, and I'm in love with him. The two are different." I nodded in agreement. "I don't know. He was just so serious when he said it."

"That isn't how you've typically heard 'I love you' in your life?"

"Not really. Usually I'll make a guy laugh. A lot. And we're in the middle of laughing and he'll say it, or we're doing something fun like riding rides at an amusement park. One guy yelled it to me while riding the Ferris wheel once. I was on the ground."

"That's pretty creative."

"Yeah. I loved it, because I could share it with the world. Or at least everyone at the fair within hearing distance."

"Yeah, I get that. So Marty's moment was…just between you two?"

"Yes."

"In bed?"

"No."

"Bonus."

"Yeah, at least I know it isn't all about what has happened there. But somehow that'd be strangely comforting—no pressure. This one was pressure. We were getting ready to go out. He finished putting his jacket and stuff on before me, so he got my gloves, hat and scarf, and put them on me, in that order. As he was wrapping the scarf, he pulled me in for a kiss with it—a long, sweet kiss. And after the kiss, he opened his eyes, looked straight into mine, and then just…said it."

"Wow. That's just about the most romantic thing I've ever heard. I never tagged Marty for the romantic type."

"I know. Neither did I. That's what made this so amazing. And so aggravating."

"Because not only did he put you on the spot, he did a perfect flipping job of it."

"He's good at perfect."

"Well, did you say it back?"

"I smiled at him, and I was silent for a moment, taking in the information after that stunner of a kiss. I hugged him, and said it into his shoulder. Of course, it was kind of muffled, so he said 'What?'"

"Oh my God, he didn't."

"He did. He totally wanted me to say it to his face. So I repeated it into his chest, and he was like 'I couldn't quite hear you… what was that?' I played through, saying 'Never mind. Since you didn't hear it the first two times, I'm sure it wasn't worth hearing.'"

"Ha! Did he tickle you until you said it, or what?"

"No, he didn't have to. He had to use the bathroom, so I went outside and wrote 'I love you, Marty!' in the snow. He saw it, and took a picture with his cell phone, and then made a comment about having to show it to the grandchildren someday."

"Oy vey."

"I know."

"No pressure or anything, eh?"

"None at all. Natalie, I started crying on the way here because I thought about it and now everything will change."

"How do you mean?"

"Well, now that my life is mostly how I want it, either he'll have to move here or I'll have to move there or we'll both have to move somewhere. I don't want to say goodbye to you and my co-workers and people I see at the store who know me and all things familiar. I don't want him to have to say goodbye to the people and things he loves either. I'm just scared."

"Well gosh Sam, it's not like he proposed already!"

"I know, but…"

"It's just around the corner, right?"

"Yeah. I can feel it. I'm scared because it's been so long since I've been in a relationship. I mean, I know what I feel is the real thing, and I'm happy, but there's a grace period for people like me. You know?"

"I know."

"And I don't need this to make me into a basket case. I know you've got your own stuff right now and I don't need to make it harder. I just had to tell someone who *gets* it."

"Yeah, Sam. Yeah. I *do* get it and I want what's best for you. So I think my best advice is to think about what would make you the happiest, and go from there. You know you want to be with him, right?"

"When he leaves, I am so sad. I miss him every minute of every day until he comes back."

"That sounds like a yes to me. You miss him not because he is fun for the weekends. You miss who he is, and what he thinks, and what he says and does and how he makes you feel. Right?"

"Right."

"Well then, would it make you happy to move with him to California, make a fresh start? Or for him to move here and make a different kind of fresh start? Or have a totally new experience for both of you, try out a different town, someplace you've always wanted to go?"

"Hmm... don't know yet," she said.

"I didn't mean you have to answer now. Just think about it. Take a day and search your soul, girl. Then talk to him when the time comes. A little soul searching is called for now and again."

"Spoken from experience, no doubt," she said.

"Indeed. At times I wish I didn't have a reason to do that, but yes."

"What's up with you?"

"Have you seen the local paper lately?"

"Which one?"

"The Herald."

"No, I don't think so."

"Oh, you would know if you'd seen it what I'm talking about. Wait, this presentation needs a visual," I said, excusing myself to jog to my car to get the paper I'd bought. I filled her in on all of it—every gory detail.

"Are you serious?"

"Unfortunately, yes."

"Have the C's seen it?"

"Not that I know of. Yet."

"Uh oh." She knew this town like I did.

"Yeah. Well, all I can do is roll with the punches," I said.

"That's true, but this was quite a punch."

"Below the belt. And the thing is I'm sure the person who took the pictures thought it'd just be a cute addition to the fire story, maybe lighten it up a little."

"And didn't think about whose life it might affect in the process."

"How would they know I wasn't the mother of those kids, right?"

"Exactly."

"Sam?"

"Yeah?"

"Do you believe everything happens for a reason?"

"I don't know. It's easier to believe when things are going right."

"No kidding. But it's hard to see things that may be right for long term, in the moment, when they feel like poo. Anyway, I'm glad we met tonight. It was meant to happen."

"Agreed."

I tried to think of a way to change the subject to something more fun. "Would you like to join me in song?"

"To be sure."

And we serenaded the empty restaurant with our best Gloria Gaynor ever, among other hits, until closing time. Oh yes, we would survive, come what may.

A Blessing in Disguise

It was Friday afternoon. I'd made it through the greater part of yet another week of misadventures. I had just put the kids down for nap. The C's had a Bose sound system, so the tunes were as cranked as they could be while I swept and mopped the kitchen floor and did the dishes. The phone rang, but the caller ID said it was a credit card company, so I ignored it. I didn't want to think about the financial issues the parents might be facing. I vacuumed the living room, and looked at the TV, which I hardly ever turned on except for kid shows, thinking today I'd pop in a movie. I'd just gotten Netflix, and the last shipment included The Pacifier. I thought maybe I could learn some tips from Vin Diesel. Maybe he knew something I didn't. I was willing to give it a try.

I enjoyed the movie immensely and had a wave of fresh new love for Vin Diesel. I'd always liked him but seeing him work with kids so well sealed the deal. I thought to myself how handy one of those wraparound packs Vin had, that held all the juices and supplies, would be in my line of work. What store carried those? Maybe I could make one, or have Sam do it. She was crafty like that.

I woke up the kids, changed a diaper, and made the afternoon snack—veggies with Ranch dressing. They enjoyed dipping them, and then realized that flicking the dip at each other was more fun. I stood by with the kitchen wipes, and told them if they didn't settle down, I would tell their parents and they would go without dinner. It seemed to work. They didn't like the "no dinner" idea too much. "Remember your manners," I said, showing them how to dunk the celery or carrot slices nicely, getting rid of excess dip before putting it in my mouth. "This is how it's done."

The father got home first and thanked me for the day. He asked how the day had gone. I gave him a full report. Then the mother got home, and asked if we could all sit down to talk.

We sat at the kitchen table, and the rest of the conversation went something like this:

"Natalie, we've been doing some thinking and we're going to have to let you go." I sat there stunned for a second, and they took this as an opportunity to continue. "We really like you. We think you're a neat girl. But the events of the past couple weeks, have been somewhat questionable."

"You think I'm a neat girl?" I shook my head. "What events? You mean Halloween?"

"Yes. You took the kids in a fire engine, into an unsafe situation. We saw the picture in the paper." Boy had I known this was coming. "They didn't have seatbelts on. They were in your lap."

"That's true, but we were in a fire engine, which happens to be one of the safest vehicles around. All other vehicles have to get out of the way, and they do, and did. Plus, we were on the way to a fire I thought you were caught in."

"But your decision to go with the firefighters in the first place..."

"Which, unfortunately, I made because of Cameron sneaking in there. Talk about unsafe. It's unsafe that your kid is always into mischief, up to no good, and never listening."

"We understand that, but it's a reputation thing. You know."

I looked at them for a moment, and realized a lot about them, all at once. These people cared about money, status, and how things looked on the surface. There was a blemish on their reputation now because of the photo in the paper. They were worried about how they would be seen in the community—their rich community.

My cell phone rang. It was Hammer. I excused myself, telling the C's I had more to say so to please wait, and went outside the front door. I told Hammer I was in the middle of something and would call him back in a half an hour, and went back inside, sat down at the table.

They said normally they'd give two weeks notice, but they just wanted to make a clean break in this instance. Fine—at least, I'd be able to get unemployment for a while, I thought.

I cleared my throat, took a deep breath, and said, "Listen. I have done my level best with your kids. I don't think they should be home together. They teach each other bad habits, which mostly is from Cameron to Courtney, although occasionally it goes the other way. I have taught your kids table manners, which were atrocious before. I have taught them how to get into the car and get right in their seats. I'm sure you've noticed."

They nodded, shocked to have this much directness coming out of me, so I figured why stop now. "Just before

Halloween, Cameron said the f-word." The mother inhaled. The father tried to hide a laugh. "I know. Let me tell you how shocking it was to hear that coming out of a 3-year-old mouth. I tried not to laugh too, but you should really do something about it if it happens again, he is three. We were getting the backpacks ready for school, and he told me his was 'too effing heavy.' I had him repeat it, to make sure I heard correctly. I asked him where he heard it. He told me he'd heard it at preschool." Personally, I knew this was a lie. He'd heard one of his parents say it, but that was beside the point. "I told him to never say that again. I told him he could choose to say it when he was forty if he wanted, because that was a grownup word and a very serious one. He hasn't used it since, at least with me. Hopefully, what I said about it being a grownup word sticks with him for a while."

I gave them a moment to absorb what I'd said, but only a moment, before I continued. "I've run after your children as they've gone separate ways while playing outside, Cameron towards the street with buses coming, Courtney towards the other end where you can't see what traffic is coming. Being one person, it's difficult to do, make a choice in that situation. I wouldn't think their parents would want me to." I paused. No answer, just their eyes staring back at me with the conviction of their decision.

"What you should also know that I didn't write in the journal is how consistent I've been with punishments and time outs, not backing down until they are broken of the bad habit. I have actually taken notice of the things they eat, and tried to change it from unhealthy most of the time and healthy once in a while to healthy most of the time with an occasional indulgence. They have tested me time and again, and I have kept with it. I've taught them the value of being efficient with time, as much as this is possible with toddlers. All the while, I've let them know they are loved and appreciated— not for what they'll do someday, but for who they *are*. They really are exceptional children, and need a lot of intellectual stimulation, and to be shown affection. Especially Cameron, who is extremely bright and energetic, and gets caught in the shadow of his cute little sister. They need structure, more than any kids I've ever babysat for."

"Well, Natalie..." the father stammered.

"About Halloween. Under the circumstances, what would you have done, thinking you the parents, who with no notice gave me their two kids for the evening, may have been injured or killed in a fire? Wouldn't you have wanted to make sure everything was all right? Or maybe you just want it to appear on the surface like it is."

I waited. They didn't say anything but were looking very guilty, and for once, I was glad.

"Who are you going to have watch them before you find a replacement?" Standing up, I didn't wait for a response. "Do you know of a good nanny? Because I do, and her name is Natalie."

With that, I turned on my heel, and walked out of the kitchen, through the front room, and out the door, which I only slammed in my head. The kids, who had been watching TV, followed me. The C's were still sitting at the table, and I saw the kids looking through the window, so I opened the door again, and hugged Cameron and Courtney tightly. "You are great kids. I love you." Then I left.

I got into my car, drove around the corner, and parked. I was hyperventilating, worse than I had at the restaurant that day. I opened the door, put my feet out and my head between my knees. My head throbbed and stomach churned. Then my phone rang.

It was Hammer. I waited a second before answering. Be strong, Natalie. Be strong.

He was excited and telling me he was leaving for a job, wanted to make sure he got in touch before he left. He'd just gotten the call and was leaving tomorrow. I listened to him describe what he'd be doing. He'd be in Florida, helping out with whatever he could. I congratulated him, and made myself breathe deeply and focus on the brilliant opportunity he had, opening up before him.

He asked how my day had been, wondering why he hadn't heard back from me, and I fibbed and told him it was the same old poop, different toilet. He laughed and said he wished he could be there to whip them into shape. You and me both, I thought. He said he couldn't get together, he had a local firefighter meeting that night, and had to pack. I told him that was fine, that we'd get together soon after he got back. That's when he said he'd be gone for two months, maybe longer. Heaven help me.

I wished him the best, and told him to be safe. That's about all I could muster with all the emotions running through me at that moment.

We hung up, and I drove to the most remote spot I could find, ran into the woods, and let it all out. Yes, I cried, but only as I punched and kicked the air. I did this for half an hour until I was covered in sweat. I started to feel better about life, but I knew I needed more.... a *lot* more. I walked to the end of the trail which I had never done before because I'd had the kids with me. There was a little gazebo, and no one was around so I sat in it and closed my eyes.

I summoned my trainer, and instantly, we were back in the garden. This time, I wore golden robes with a purple sash in the middle, made of very soft material. I wanted to ask if I could have with some of these cool clothes after our meeting was over, but I thought better of it. He wore dark green robes of the same material with a gold sash. We were color coordinated.

He smiled at me. He always looked like he already knew what I'd been going through, but this time he really looked like he knew.

"Hello, Phoenix," he said.

"Hello, trainer." I bowed. "Thanks for meeting me. Sorry to disturb you."

"It's okay. It's a benefit of being the gym owner. I can leave whenever I please. Unless of course if I'm teaching a class."

"Which I was 99% sure you weren't, right now."

He asked me to stand up. I stood up. He walked over to me, putting his hands on my shoulders. "You are very strong. You've been through a lot. I've been watching."

"You can see what happens to me?"

"If I try. And only if I use it for the highest good with pure intention, much like yourself. I was worried about you, always trying to conquer the world as you do. So I spied on you a couple times." He laughed. I laughed with him. Under different circumstances, I might've been suspicious of what he saw when he visited, but not in this one. Not with him. I trusted him implicitly.

"So you saw what happened today?"

"Yes."

I bowed my head. I didn't want him to see my defeat. "I don't know what to say."

"Natalie, do you feel you did your best with these children?"

"Yes."

"Then there is nothing to be ashamed of. I know you did your best. I *saw*. It doesn't take a genius or a psychic to see that you have a good heart, and that you are a very good babysitter."

"Thank you, teacher." I was so glad he believed in me.

"You are welcome."

"I am ashamed of the way I spoke to the parents before I left." I paused, eyeing him. "You saw that too?"

"Yes. I don't know why you're ashamed."

"Well, respecting your elders."

"Sometimes our elders don't act like elders. Quite often, this is the case. And I would say these parents, the C's as you call them, are definitely more like kids most of the time. They didn't want to accept responsibility for creating the monsters, so they placed the blame on you."

"True, even though I was only with them for a matter of months."

"Yes."

"Thank you for your assessment of the situation. It matches my own, but it feels different, being inside the situation. I thought maybe I was just biased."

"Not at all. Natalie, there is something I want to convey. I was going to visit even if you didn't call on me tonight, to tell you. You have become quite an accomplished martial artist, and you have many talents, which you are just beginning to realize." I didn't quite know what he meant by this. He saw the question in my eyes. "I see things in your future that will make you very happy. Telling you any more than that is breaking the rules, and would have dire consequences for both of us."

I sat in awe of him, this shining soul who had been my mentor for two years. I felt very blessed. Of course, curiosity was in there in the rolodex of feelings too, but I didn't push. Dire consequences weren't something I'd wish on anyone. My eyes filled with tears. I knew this would be an emotional weekend.

"I understand."

"Now go, live your life. Don't waste another precious minute feeling an ounce of guilt. Let the C's take that on."

"Okay. I respect and honor you, trainer." We bowed. I closed my eyes, and suddenly smelled cloves. I opened my eyes to decipher the origin of the scent, and Jin was gone.

"Likewise, my student. Enjoy the beauty that is all around you," his voice said, echoing from somewhere, far away, but still close. I'd have to learn those vocal tricks someday.

I realized I was still there in the garden and hadn't popped back to reality like last time. Permission to explore the grounds—granted. Too cool!

I walked around for a while, over a hill, and saw a Pagoda. I had always wanted to see one up close, ever since childhood in Japan. Here was my chance. I wondered if there was anyone inside.

There was a shimmering pool with goldfish swimming around in it. I watched them for a moment—all different colors of them, but different than I'd ever seen—purples, blues and greens. They seemed to be all parts of the same huge fish, so fluid—unlike bumbling goldfish I'd seen, these didn't bump into each other. They had flow.

A voice startled me out of my daze. It was a woman's voice, soft and smooth. "Excuse me." I turned to look, and saw the most ethereally beautiful Japanese woman I'd ever seen. She had hair down to her waist and a smile that lit up her face. Her skin was a half shade lighter than other Asian people I had met. "I am half Japanese, and half white," she said, explaining. I was taken aback. She could read my thoughts. I had better be careful what I think. She was fragile, yet firm. Strong. She was my height, and she wore a white tank top, long white skirt, and filmy yellow blouse. I couldn't help smiling back at her. "I've been waiting for you. Please, come inside."

I wondered if she had the right person. "I'm not supposed to be here," I stammered.

"Yes you are, Natalie," she said, her hand on my elbow, guiding me. I smiled. Nothing should surprise me anymore, but somehow, certain things still did. She led me into the foyer of the building. I was awestruck by the architecture. I thought it would feel somewhat claustrophobic, but it wasn't. The ceiling was tiered, of course, but painted the same shade of pale yellow as the woman's blouse. Every other tier was pale blue, providing pleasant contrast. The colors made the ceiling seem open.

There was a fireplace, which I don't think had real fire but it looked real. We walked past a greenhouse to a glass elevator. It opened as we approached it, and we took it up two levels. The doors opened, and we walked towards a room with a blue door. She pushed a code on the outside, and it opened into the wall with a swoosh, like in Star Trek.

We walked through, and I saw two yoga mats unrolled on the floor. One had a dragon on it, the other a Japanese symbol which I recognized as the symbol for harmony. She pointed to the latter and said it was for me. "Would you like to do yoga before your massage?" she asked.

Whoa, this afternoon came with a massage too? I should get fired more often! "Okay," I said, trying to roll with this experience, although I didn't know what on earth I was doing here. I thought I had only summoned my trainer, not a health spa.

We sat in meditation for ten minutes, and spoke without ever opening our mouths. She said I would have to search my soul now, but the answer would come to me before long. She told me to lie on my back, and she lay on her mat. We did a chakra opening exercise, and then she taught me how to open my heart involving a deep exhale with hands in prayer position and then opening out, saying it was a good practice to start the day and end the day.

She told me everything that'd happened was for the purpose of my evolution. She said she'd been observing the events of my life since I was a child, because she knew I would advance to this point, but that I belonged somewhere else.

"Thank you for all you've told me. Who are you?" I asked.

"I'm sorry," she said. "I forgot to introduce myself. My name is Jade." She didn't give herself a label, or a job title, just Jade. I was okay with that. She was very godly, so if she said she was goddess, I probably couldn't have handled that. It would have blown my poor stressed out mind. Jade was just fine.

"Do you know my trainer?"

"Yes." And that was that. She didn't expand on it, explain herself, or expend any extra energy. I felt like asking her his name, but then thought better of it. I had a feeling the Universe probably didn't want to be tested, and wasn't about to test my theory.

"It is what you need right now, to be here, to be with me."

"Thank you."

"You're welcome, Phoenix," she said, smiling. I looked into her eyes, and could see the humor there. She had been reading me as I doubted her.

"I'm sorry," I said. "It's my training. It has taught me to trust no one immediately."

"This is understandable. Most humans don't deserve automatic trust," she said, rising.

"Am I going to spar, here?" I asked.

"No. This is simply your healing place. Today you got an expanded view. There is more, and it will be here any time you wish to visit. I will be here, waiting." Tears filled my eyes, and my heart filled with gratitude. "Now it is time for your massage."

We left the Pagoda, and she led me outside to another room, with windows on all sides like a meditation room, but in the shape of a hexagon. We were just inside a forest now, and it felt very safe. The sun shone through the trees, and all kinds of animals walked around outside, free of fear. She told me that Colin, the massage therapist, would join me soon, and that I should take off my robe and get under the blanket. I did so. Somehow, with her, I wasn't embarrassed. I lay on my stomach, already melting into the massage table.

She kissed my forehead, told me she'd see me soon, and left. Colin came in. He reminded me of someone, but I wasn't sure who. He was thin with glasses and a diamond-shaped face. He was of Asian descent, but had green eyes... very striking. His eyes sought into me, where I needed healing and he did what he called a chakra-cleansing massage with hot stones going up my back, telling me to focus on the certain colors that corresponded with the chakras. He told me it would help me interact with the world with fresh energy during my new beginning. He told me to turn over, which I did, and he did some tension release techniques on my neck and shoulders. He said I should get dressed, left the room, and came back several minutes later with a green smoothie. I was somewhat timid about drinking it, but he told me the ingredients, which were all natural. I trusted him, so I drank it—delicious. I thanked him. "It is an herbal remedy that you can make for yourself any time you feel too much stress."

We walked out into the woods, through a path and to the edge of the ocean. "I didn't know I could get to the ocean from Pagodaland," I said.

"Here it is. Enjoy it. I hope to see you again soon." He walked back along the path. I walked along, sipping my smoothie, for what felt like hours. Finally, I got tired so I sat there looking at the waves for a while, and then lay down and looked up at the sky, remembering what a big world it was after all. I closed my eyes, feeling more at peace than I had in a long, long time.

Christmas Presence and Presents

When I woke up, I was in my very own bed. How had I gotten there? I hadn't driven home after work. Obviously, I'd have to get used to this disappearing and reappearing somewhere else thing. Right now, after making sure my car was in its parking space, I wasn't too concerned. I felt relaxed and at peace. The reality of how I was going to pay my bills next month hadn't hit yet. I had more important things to figure out, like how to tell Sam. I would tell Hammer too, but not until I knew he was close to coming home.

I dialed and got her voicemail, so I just asked her to give me a call. Then I just had to clean. I cleaned my kitchen, bathroom, living room, and bedroom. I vacuumed, dusted, swept, mopped, polished, and I probably would've cleaned the gutters on my apartment building if it hadn't already been done. After I finished with my apartment, I got started on myself. I showered, dried off, lotioned up, turned on my curling iron, dried my hair, primped, primed, polished, pressed, got dressed, curled my hair, and checked messages.

Sam had called back saying she'd be free tonight if I wanted to go out, so I called her and arranged to meet her in an hour.

On the way, I text messaged Hammer asking if he was up to his ass in alligators. I was anxious to see how he was doing and even more anxious to know how long 'til he got back. He texted back, said he was doing fine, but that he wouldn't be back for a month and a half. That meant just before Christmas. I wrote that I missed him, closed the phone and walked into the restaurant before the tears could start.

The truth was, I really, *really* missed him. Living in the moment was great, having no attachments was great, but some moments were so painful to live through alone. I was glad I had Sam. She was one of the few who really got it. Since my parents had been killed in a boating accident when I was 16, I needed a shoulder to cry on, and sometimes, guidance. I'd been on my own since then. Not many people knew that about me, or deciphered it like Hammer had.

That's part of the reason I wanted to hold off on having kids. I knew the feeling of being left behind, and never wanted that to be my kids' story, just in case something happened to me. Sam knew it was my story. She didn't mother me, and I didn't want her to, but she knew when I needed support.

She'd just gotten there too, so we sat and ordered our usual.

"You called this meeting right after we just got together, so I know something's up," she said.

I 'fessed up about the firing. She looked at me in complete shock, asking why. I explained how it was all about the article, and the family's status in the community although they had claimed it was my decision to take the kids to the fire. I told her what I said to them and how I walked out. She high fived me for my parting words and then just sat there shaking her head.

"That's just wrong," she finally said.

"I agree," I said.

"It's stuff you didn't put there, that got you into trouble in the first place. The pulling the fire alarm, and everything else those little brats did. They've had two and three years to learn their bad habits, behavior, and lately, language."

"I know. I can't reverse the damage. I only hope the next nanny has more luck or knows how to reach them."

"She might know how to reach them, but so do you. You've told me how you get them singing and encourage them to be themselves, in addition to using all the little tricks and distractions when they don't listen or start testing you. I don't see someone being able to do that any better than you, even with 10 *years* of experience. Hell, I don't see Nanny Mc-Freaking-Phee being able to deal with these monsters."

"Well, thank you and neither do I, though I've wished for a magic stick like hers so many times, but the combination of me and these kids was not meant to be, I guess." I thought about it for a moment, and said, "Maybe I should call Mrs. Doubtfire."

Sam laughed. "Doubt…fire."

"Exactly," I said.

"What're you going to do to make money?"

"I don't know yet. Maybe get a temp job. That's really the only thing I can think of. I could get a seasonal job, with the holidays coming up. That'll keep food on the table and me busy. I can do espresso, I've done that before."

"You'll find something," she said. "Wait, we have an opening at the bank. One of the girls is leaving to have a baby!"

"Thanks, but I royally suck at numbers. Math was my worst subject. I pay my bills, but that's all the number crunching I care to do. I'll find something, really."

"I know. You always land on your feet."

I hoped she was right. Right now, I didn't know where I was going, and I didn't really care, at least for this evening. I wanted to enjoy being with my friend, and that's exactly what I did.

"All I know is, Sam, this is going to require a lot of Vin Diesel."

She laughed. "Get this girl some Vin, stat!"

So we rented several of the Fast & the Furious series, Chronicles of Riddick, A Man Apart, XXX, and Pitch Black. We got through a few that evening, with popcorn. It was an excellent main course. The others we saved for dessert.

The next day, I spent 3 hours at the gym, working off my frustrations and practicing martial arts technique. The firefighters were there, and asked me how everything was going. I said fine. I didn't want Hammer to catch word of my being 86'd, or any of them to feel like they had to come to my rescue. Not this time. I was going to get myself out of it.

The rainy weather didn't help my mood, which would waver between the relief of not having to deal with tantrums and change diapers, and remorse that I'd lost a job I was good at doing. Plus I was sure that I'd let Yoda down and that made me sad. Even so, I did things to keep myself cheerful.

I baked chocolate chip cookies, oatmeal chocolate chip cookies, peanut butter cookies, snicker doodles, and sugar cookies. When I was done baking, I put the ingredients away, the utensils in the dishwasher, and looked at the stash. I had approximately 200 cookies. I looked at the cookies, and figured I better put them in Christmas tins, which I conveniently had in the closet. Then I got tired of thinking about cookies, so I got out my yoga mat. While doing yoga, I had a little thought bubble pop: those firefighters could probably use the sugar high to keep them going and would definitely burn the calories faster than I could. So, I teleported myself and the many, many cookies down to the station. (Hey, I had to have some fun with this. After all, I was still using my gift for the greatest good. ☺) Seeing the look on their faces gave me a natural high. Tim hugged me and asked how Hammer was doing.

I told him I'd been in contact with him a couple days ago and it sounded like Hammer was doing great. I agreed to pass along the greeting when I spoke to him next. He asked how I was doing, searching my face. I fibbed and told him I was just fine. He paused for a moment, like he was sensing something was up, but decided not to pry, which was good because I didn't know what I'd say. I hadn't thought of an excuse for having free time yet.

After getting some groceries, I went home and put them away. It had been a nice little vacation week, and having more time to spend at the gym was lovely, but I was starting to wonder where rent would come from. I had saved some money from my prior nanny job (because that family had paid me entirely too much), but had designated those funds for Christmas presents.

I was so worn out from working out an extra hour that I curled up on the couch. I heard purring beside me, and scratched my cat behind the ears and under the chin. She loved that. "Kiki, what am I going to do?" I asked.

"I don't know Natalie, but you better figure it out. I don't want to ssstarve," she said, in her high-pitched meowing voice. I laughed. She kind of had the lisping thing going on like Sylvester, when he said "Suffering succotash."

I must be dreaming. Usually I didn't realize I was dreaming when actually doing so, but today I did. Well, hot diggety dog, a lucid dream! If I had a talking cat, I was going to get some answers.

"Don't worry Kiki, you won't starve. But you could be a constructive kitty, and help me choose a career path." Kiki, being a Zen cat, would have some sage advice for me. I knew she would.

"I don't know. Instead of being able to disappear, I wish you would've gotten a mmmore useful talent."

"Like what? Making fresh salmon appear on your dinner plate every night?"

She p'shawed me with her paw. "Mmmnooo. You know what I mmmean," she said. "You could have been bestowed with the talent of seeing fires before they happen, and preventing them. Or catching arsonists."

"Wouldn't want to put the firefighters out of business, now would we?" I asked.

"Nnnno, meow. It was just a thought. Salmmmon is acceptable."

"You're a bit more of a smartass than I expected you to be."

"Sereow...serious will cost you extra."

"What are we talking?"

"Mmmmmew...Krispy Kremes for Christmas."

"You drive a hard bargain, Keekster."

"Desperate times call for desperate meowww... measures."

"Alright already, you'll have your Krispy Kremes. Then will you tell me your thoughts?"

"Mmmeow... maybe."

"Okay, we'll go over and get some as soon as we can," I promised. I couldn't believe I just promised my cat doughnuts. I thought about going over to the store because it wouldn't require a trip across the water, but Kiki would know I cheated, and I didn't want the wrath of Kiki on my hands. The Wrath of Kiki... it could be a movie. I giggled at the hilarity of it, and woke myself up laughing. Kiki sat on my chest, looking at me pointedly.

"Wait," I said. "What did you just ask me for?"

...No answer.

"Oh well, I guess I just dreamed it," I said.

Kiki made a huffy nasal sound, jumped down, and slinked off to the bedroom. I was hoping I'd make her talk. That way, I could get us on one of those animal shows and make a fortune, but it was not to be.

I hadn't even been able to ask her why exactly cats hated water so much, who her heroes were, whether she preferred beef, chicken or tuna Friskies, or if she had ever known a feline to be a vegetarian. Bummer.

Kiki was right, you know. I should've gotten a more useful talent than disappearing. I mean, how useful could that be to society? When things got rough, Ninja Nanny... disappeared? I mean, it was cool that I could save lives that way, but I needed to see if I had other talents, and at least develop the one I had. I wasn't sure how to do that, but I figured I'd visit my happy place, the Pagoda, later, and see what they had to tell me. Until then, I was going to take some steps toward employment in the real world. I had already received the unemployment paperwork, but hoped I wouldn't have to use that money.

I opened the classifieds. I knew I wasn't moving away from here unless it meant a warmer climate, so I didn't bother looking in the big city. I was just too accustomed to the slower pace that my town provided. I didn't think I could handle office jobs for long, but I applied, grudgingly, to a few of those online. There were a couple other nanny positions, but I knew the families they were for and my nanny reputation was soiled around here. Even if that wasn't the case, it would just be too awkward, bumping into the other family at gymnastics or the park.

Then I saw a coffee job available. It was part time, mornings from 7:30-noon, Monday through Friday. I dialed the phone number, and immediately recognized the voice. His name may be Elliot, but to me he would forever be the Lollipop Man. I asked him about the job, and he said experience was required, though it didn't have to be recent. Perfect. He told me to come on down and make some drinks, show him what I had.

I pulled up at the drive through, said hello and told him I had called about the job.

"I know. I recognized your voice," he said, smiling. "Come on in and I'll make you a drink."

So I parked, went in and he made me the best mocha I'd ever had. "We switched to a mix of milk with Torani syrup, to add to the chocolate," he said, observing the blissful expression cross my face.

"I approve," I said happily.

"How about you make me a French Vanilla Latte?"

"You got it." I looked around and noticed there wasn't French Vanilla flavoring. Aah, a test. I found the regular vanilla and the hazelnut; poured half a shot of each, made him the best Frenchie I'd ever made, and got the job.

He refreshed my memory about everything, and then we went through cleaning and closing procedure. I wouldn't have to lock up, but he showed me that too, just in case. It all looked simple, and they didn't actually cook any food so that was a bonus. They just served muffins and scones, no fancy stuff. They had all kinds of flavored Chai and made Chai shakes and fruit smoothies. He showed me where the doggie bones were and where to dump the coffee grounds.

We could have one free drink per shift and were allowed the day old baked goods, but had to pay for the fresh ones. It sounded fair to me. I knew they didn't make a huge amount of money, and now, neither would I so I was cool with day old baked goods. Free breakfast worked for me. Tips were all mine for my shift because I'd be the only one on it.

"What happened to your last barista?" I asked. "The one I saw working with you sometimes when I drove by?"

"She got a full time job doing medical filing," he said. "That was my daughter. Well, one of them," he grinned.

"Oh, really? Well if she's doing what she loves, I guess it's better for her."

"And for me. She didn't enjoy making coffee."

"Well that's not me. After those kids, coffee is heaven."

"Yeah, what happened? Did they drive you away and finally force you to quit?"

"Nope. I got fired," I said, shaking my head.

"For what?"

I explained the whole thing that'd happened on Halloween and what I'd told the C's on my way out the door. He agreed that it was bogus, and said he was glad to have me for however long I would stay. I thanked him for the opportunity. I didn't know what I was going to do to make enough to pay bills, because this job, with tips, would just about pay my rent. But I was sure I'd figure something out.

I got through the first two weeks without any fires, floods, earthquakes, tornadoes, or other natural disasters, cataclysms, or catastrophes. When the firefighters stopped by for coffee, including Tim, I knew I had to call Hammer and tell him before he caught wind of it from them. They asked me what had happened, and I said I'd had a difference of opinion with the parents—which wasn't a lie, I just didn't feel like telling them that my being fired had anything to do with the fire.

Tim said he'd be thrilled to see me every day, wished me well, and dropped two dollars into the tip jar. He was such a sweet man.

After my shift ended I immediately went home, got my workout clothes, and headed to the gym to do some martial arts. On the way, I called Hammer and came clean with what'd happened. He listened while I explained the parents' reasoning. I didn't tell him what I said when I was fired or what I thought of it, because I wanted to know his thoughts.

"Wow."

"Yeah..."

"Well, I have to say it's a bunch of bull that you got fired. Those kids are too much for one person to handle and their parents should acknowledge that fact."

"Thanks for that." I felt better knowing he saw things from my point of view on this.

"I'm sorry things turned out this way, babe. I know the kids will miss you. Like you though, I believe everything happens for a reason. So are you looking for another job?"

"Well, actually I already got one, a part timer," I said, telling him about the coffee job and that I'd seen Tim today.

"Cool. Is it enough to get the bills paid?"

"Not quite," I said. "But I'm looking for something to top it off."

"I'll think about it and see what I come up with."

"Thanks." Just then, the cell phone beeped, and I saw that someone was calling in so I said goodbye to Hammer and answered it. It turned out to be Cameron and Courtney's neighbor from across the street, asking if I could babysit that night. That one took me by surprise, because I didn't know they would even consider me after I'd been fired from their friends' house.

They had a 4-year-old girl, Maddie, and a baby boy, Brendan. Cameron and Courtney had played with them a couple times so we were familiar. I thought they were sweet. I figured they'd lead me down the primrose path like Cameron and Courtney had, drawing me in with cuteness until I found out they really had the "Devil Inside." Plus, there was the detail of my previous family living across the street, and it was a total cookie cutter neighborhood, with no privacy whatsoever. As if reading my mind, the mother suggested that I park in their garage. I accepted. I was to show up at 7pm—perfect, it'd already be dark since winter was fully upon us.

I did half an hour of yoga at the gym, and felt refreshed. It was great to have the downstairs all to myself when I needed it. There were no windows in the Chi Club since it was in the basement, but there was a wood floor and the walls were painted a nice pale yellow, so it seemed light anyway. I lay on my mat, eyes closed and felt myself floating. I knew I should get up, but found that I couldn't move. My breathing deepened and I began to drift.

This time, I arrived by boat. It wasn't a cruise ship, or even a yacht, or even a canoe like the one Hammer and I tipped. It was a rowboat. I was in a rowboat in the open ocean, but I had no oar. I giggled up to the big blue sky, wondering if this was symbolic of something, if I should be learning something, or if it was just a cosmic joke. I didn't hear any voices directing me to do anything, so I took it as a sign to go with the flow and let the boat make its way to the shore.

I disembarked, pulled my boat up onto the dry sand where the water didn't reach, and headed for the Pagoda. I knew which direction to go in, somehow, even though it just looked like a long stretch of beach with no houses or other landmarks to guide me. About 20 minutes later, I found the trail leading to the massage building and the Pagoda. I paused by the pond, thinking about what I'd come here for this time.

I'm not sure how long I stood there, but I felt an arm around each side of my waist. Jin was standing on one side and on the other side stood Jade. I smiled. They greeted me, this time without speaking. I could hear their voices in my head.

"Natalie, welcome back."

"Thank you. I came by boat this time."

"I guess you were supposed to, for some reason." Jade's eyes twinkled. I just looked at her, wondering what she knew that I didn't. Probably quite a lot.

"Let's have tea," my trainer said.

"Yes, Sifu. Thank you."

We went into a large, open room with terraced stairs and sat in the middle on a blanket, where there was a low table. We each had our own pillow to sit on. They were an amber color. I was learning a lot about cool furniture and décor from these meetings.

"You have questions," Jin said.

"Yes. Well, one, specifically," I said.

"We'll do our best."

"If you've looked at my life lately, you know it's been a bit of a struggle financially. I got a coffee job and am scheduled to do some babysitting tonight."

"Yes, we know."

"Am I wasting my energy by dividing my time like this? Chi is hard to come by these days. I feel so drained."

"You've been through a lot," Jade said. "You've bounced back remarkably well in a short time. The way of the warrior is not always straight. The path has unforeseen challenges."

"So you're advising me to stay where I am and see what happens?"

"For now. You have a source of income. You can supplement that with the babysitting and if that's not enough, there are other things you can do. Temporary work of one kind or another. House cleaning, for example, is good exercise and can be very therapeutic."

"This is true. Thanks, I'll look into it. I'm also wondering if I have other talents or skills besides the disappearing."

They both smiled. "This, Natalie, you have to find out in time. You have to do your own evolving. If we tell you what you are able to do, you will either be frustrated because you aren't able to do it yet, or you might limit yourself to only that, or not set your sights higher. Therefore, the powers you possess are for you to discover."

"So, you're saying there is something?"

"We can only tell you this: Yes, there is more to the story."

"Excellent." This news thrilled me. If nothing else, I'd gotten confirmation that I was capable of more than I had done thus far. It fueled me to continue on my path—practicing The Way. Not that I needed one. I knew I had made a good choice for myself when I started martial arts.

I thanked them. "You're welcome," they said in unison.

Suddenly, I was back in the boat. I hadn't even had to walk back to it and pull it down the sand to the water. I was just in it. I smiled, figuring this was their way of showing me what was possible. Still no oars—not even any popsicle sticks—but the sky was blue with no signs of storm. Hard as it was for me to relax, I had so little time to do so in life. So I reclined back, lulled to sleep like a baby in the cradle of the gentle waves, knowing this place would always be here for me, and that nothing bad could happen to me here; a place of solace in a frenzied world. I let the arms of the ocean hold and rock me there a while longer, and when ready, I returned.

That evening, I watched baby Brendan's eyes close. In two minutes, he was asleep, so peacefully. He had gone down early, and now there was one.

Maddie smiled up at me and took my hand, leading me into the kitchen. She went and got a pad of paper and a pen. "What'll it be today?"

"I don't know yet, I'm not finished looking at the menu."

"Take your time," she said, waving her hand and walking back behind the counter.

A few minutes later, I signaled her that I was ready. "I'll have a hamburger, French fries, and a chocolate shake." She scribbled madly on the page.

"Anything for dessert?"

"Yes. I'll have a slice of lemon meringue pie and some coffee. Can I have dessert first?"

"Coming right up, ma'am."

"Thanks. You're a good waitress. I'm going to give you a good tip."

"I need it. I have so many bills!"

I giggled, thinking she must've heard this from her parents—a natural mimic, and perhaps an actress later in life.

She went down 30 minutes later. There had been so little fuss, just a tiny bit of whining and that was all she had for me. I couldn't believe how easy these kids were! I went to the kitchen, tidied up, made myself a snack and headed for the living room to relax. Then I thought twice and opened the cabinet door where the kids' plates and bowls were. I had to smile. Just as I thought: no cartoon plates, bowls or silverware, just simple pastel colors—two of each. I liked this family already.

The rest of the evening was quiet. I had time to think about Christmas, which was only two weeks away. Thanksgiving had passed uneventfully for me, because Sam had her family and Hammer was still gone. I'd been invited to share it with a couple other friends, but declined, preferring the peace of doing yoga instead of the bloat from overeating.

I thought about what I'd get everyone, starting with those who had helped me through the past several stressful months. I wanted to get my trainer something he would love, but that wouldn't take up too much space. I could tell he was a minimalist. I was sure his home had good Feng Shui and no clutter. For him I would go to the local import shop where there were always good decorative gifts and candles that smelled heavenly. I finished making my list, and checked on the kids. Sound asleep. Maybe I could drift off for a bit before their parents got home too. I felt my body sink into the big fluffy chair.

A thump from outside startled me awake. Were they home already? I could've sworn I'd only been asleep a few minutes. I checked my watch and validated that. It had only been 10 minutes, and I saw no headlights, heard no footsteps. I got up to check it out.

Peeking out the front window onto the porch, I saw nothing. No one in the yard. I opened the door, and stepped out into the cold, crisp, dry evening air. No rain was rare for this season, and I savored every minute of it. I thought rain should only happen from midnight to 6am, everywhere on the planet. It could rain as hard as it wanted to, as long as it only did it after I was asleep and before I woke up. If I wanted to, then I could stay up on the rare occasions when rain was wanted. Otherwise, I thought my rule should be instated.

A rustling in the bushes attracted my eyes. "Who's there?" No answer, just more rustling. I shined my keychain flashlight on the bushes and a familiar pair of eyes stared out at me. They seemed to be crinkled at the outer corners, like a smile. It was Wanda. "Well, you little rascal! You scared me. You could've at least answered when I asked who it was."

No reply. Damn, this one couldn't be tricked into talking either. I walked towards him to pick him up, and he darted. I could've sworn I heard a giggle, but I'm sure that was just my imagination...right?

I followed him across the street to Cameron and Courtney's house. I knew I was treading into dangerous territory here, but what could I do? This was an inside cat. I wasn't about to knock on their door, but I could at least put him safely on their porch. He wouldn't stay, but at least that way I would know I did my part to ensure his safety.

He walked the perimeter of the house. I followed. It was interesting, stalking a cat. The hunter became the hunted. As long as he didn't go up on the roof, we were cool. I followed him as he crept behind the kids' backyard play area, and stopped on the other side of the house to sniff some plants. I knew if I walked slowly, he wouldn't dart away, and then I could go in for the grab swiftly. I stood in wait for him to get nice and comfortable, and was distracted by a movement inside the window. Mom was doing dishes. She looked absolutely exhausted. I heard kids' voices. Up late tonight, were they? Well, that was interesting. She had told me they were always in bed by 8pm sharp—weekdays and weekends. I backed up from the window and pushed the Indiglo button on my watch. 9:30pm. Hmm.

They had been eating, and she let them out of their chairs. Cameron could unfasten his booster seat himself, but Courtney couldn't so Camalia let her out. I could see the kids' heads bobbing up and down next to their mother. They were jumping and laughing loudly. I could see Camalia losing patience, and Carl not coming to the rescue.

Wanda was on the move again, so I kept my eyes on him, but there was no way I could get past that window without being seen. Or was there? I closed my eyes, and suddenly I was in front of the house, facing Wanda directly. "Gotcha," I smiled, scooping him up. Now, I had to figure out how to get him to stay on the porch. The breeze was picking up, and I wanted to go back across the street before the parents came back. "Wanda, you stay here."

He sniffed, haughtily. That wasn't going to happen, I could tell. "Alright, butthead, then we're going in." I wondered if I could pull this off. I mean, what if I disappeared and appeared in the middle of the kitchen where the mother and kids were? That just wouldn't be satisfactory at all. I couldn't have the press involved in my disappearing and reappearing act—no way, no how. I would have to remember to ask my trainer if I could disappear and stay disappeared when I got to my destination, or if I always had to become visible again. I saw an upstairs light go on: the hall light. Then Cameron's light—on, off. Then, a few minutes later, Courtney's—on, off. Then the master bedroom light went on, and I figured that's how it would stay for a while. All downstairs lights were off except the main entry one and that was always left on.

"Alright, kitty, here we go! Hold on!" If only I had Scotty to beam me up or a port key like Harry Potter. In real life, I guess we had to do transport ourselves. I held onto Wanda, squeezed my eyes shut, and took a deep breath.

I opened my eyes. I was in. Right in front of the coat rack where I'd hung my jacket zillions of times. "That was easier than I thought," I whispered. I put Wanda down, and he ran towards his food bowl in the laundry room. I looked around, and decided lingering would be a bad idea. I closed my eyes, and when I opened them, I was outside again. I could have fun with this! But I really should get back.

In the middle of the street, I had a sudden brainstorm. If the family had gotten a new nanny, which I was sure they would've by now, she might be staying above the garage in the nanny apartment—the one I'd never used because I had my own place. I turned around. Sure enough—there was a reading light on up there.

I waited, turning it over and over in my mind. To go, or not to go? What if she spotted me? I didn't want to give the poor girl a heart attack, just wanted to check her out, see what my replacement was like. Unfortunately I couldn't fly, so I couldn't just peek in the window, or could I? There was only one way to find out.

My trainer had said I could only use my powers for the highest possible good. Well, this qualified, didn't it? I mean, I wanted to make sure the new nanny was a good person and babysitter, vibe her a little.

I decided it was now or never. No sign of the parents coming home across the street. I closed my eyes, crossed my fingers, and aimed for outside the window. I opened them, and I hadn't moved. So much for the flying idea. Maybe that would happen later, although I would rather be able to breathe underwater.

I aimed for the stairwell. That was out of view of the bed, and I could just show up for a moment, take a peek, and leave.

I opened my eyes. I wasn't in the stairwell. I was in... where was I? It was dark. The closet? No, no clothes. I was in her bathroom!

Luckily, she wasn't also in her bathroom and luckily, the door was cracked. I peered out. She was in bed, which was actually a futon mattress on the floor, but not reading. She was talking on the phone, or listening to someone talk actually. She had long, straight brown hair and brown eyes, and struck me as sort of hippyish, in her mid-30's. She opened her mouth and started speaking. Yes, definitely a flower child out of her era. She talked about what had happened that day with the kids. "It drove me nuts, dude!" she said. "They kept asking 'why' to everything. I have never met such spoiled brats in all my years of babysitting."

I stifled a giggle. I felt her pain.

"You know me. Usually I'm pretty laid back, right? I mean, nothing gets to me and I can let things roll off pretty easily. Well not with these kids! I can't turn my back on them for a second!"

I'd heard enough. I was sure the kids were in good hands. The new nanny had her work cut out for her, but she would probably smoke enough stuff to calm herself down. I could smell it, and wanted to advise her to light some incense so the parents wouldn't, but I couldn't really do that without freaking her out. In fact, it was about time I got back. The other parents were due home soon and I didn't want to take any chances. I looked around the room at the sparse decorations, and then noted with interest that my pirate ship had been moved up here. So maybe the kids were allowed to come up and play sometimes. I beamed myself into the living room across the street.

Everything was in order. I'd been gone only a few minutes, but it felt like longer. I got myself a glass of ice water and fell asleep watching TV. From within my stupor, I heard the faint sound of the door opening, and felt a hand on my shoulder. The mother asked if everything had gone okay, and I said yes, telling her how Brendan had gone right down and Maddie had been my waitress. As for the other stuff involving Wanda, I thought it best to leave that out. She paid me, and I went happily home, thinking that all this time, the perfect family for me to nanny had been right across the street. Go figure!

Sam and I met at our favorite restaurant to exchange Christmas gifts. It was the week before Christmas, but this was our way of making the joy last a little longer. We hadn't talked in a while, besides rare moments when I stopped at the bank, so I asked her how things were going with Marty.

"That's what I was going to tell you tonight," she said, eyeing me.

"What's up?"

"He wants me to move to California."

"Really? Are you going to?" I waited, anxious.

"I'm not sure yet. I would have to leave you, my dear BFF, and find a job down there."

"Don't want to let him support you, huh?"

"Ahem, no. Although he easily could with his salary, and probably wouldn't mind, I would be bored out of my mind. Plus, I'm more women's lib than that."

"Yeah, I know."

"I guess I wanted to bounce it off of you, get your thoughts."

"Well, personally and selfishly, I would love for you to stay. But realistically and objectively, I know you want to move on, make babies, live in the sun."

She looked at me, smiling with tears in her eyes and nodded her head. "I do. I never thought I would ever admit it in eight billion years, but I do." The tears made her eyes sparkle.

"Oh, Sam," I said. "It is totally understandable. I'm ecstatic for you! And I'm sure you can find a job in a bank down there, if even just part time."

"That's true," she said, looking slightly mysterious. "That's not exactly all I have to tell you."

"There's more?"

"He proposed."

I grabbed her hands in excitement. "OhmiGod! Really? When, how?" He hadn't been here for a while, so I hoped he hadn't done it over the phone.

"He sent me a CD in the mail. It said, in big blocky letters, "Open me and play me in the car in the parking lot of the bank before work no sooner or later than the morning of 12/20. Love, Marty." Right then I was suspicious. No idea what the boy was up to."

"So..."

"So I got to the bank, and popped it in. It played the song *In Your Eyes* by Peter Gabriel. I listened to the whole thing. He knew I loved that movie, Say Anything, and the moment where John Cusack holds up the stereo to her window. I was already emotional, but then he had recorded his voice on the CD:

"I put that on there because I couldn't be here, holding up the stereo to your window. After all, you live on the first floor. Sam, I love you more than I've ever loved any woman."

"Then I heard a tap on my window. He was standing there, beside my car."

"Whaaat!?!?! Wow!"

"I know! He flew into town just for this. He knew what time I got to work. I rolled down my window, at a loss for words. I opened my mouth to try, but couldn't speak.

He opened my car door, and got down on one knee, which was extra touching, because it was raining. Then he asked me, and gave me a beautiful ring. I said yes. I have never wanted anything so much in my life."

I was crying by now. I didn't know Mr. Martypants had it in him. "What did you say?"

"I said yes. I got out of my car, and he spun me around and around in the parking lot in his arms. And apparently, he'd had some help from the girls at the bank, because they gave us a standing ovation from just outside the door."

"Perfect," I said. "Just like a movie."

"Better." She showed me her ring. It was the most exquisite thing I had ever seen—the ring itself, gold and silver entwined, with a diamond shaped like a crescent moon, with two tiny stars, one silver and one gold. Sam had always loved the moon.

"It's beautiful," I said. The ring had taken my breath away. I hugged Sam. We were both wiping tears from our eyes when the waitress came, noticing the ring and emotions overflowing from our table.

"Oh my God, congratulations!" she said, hugging Sam. She was our favorite waitress. Sam thanked her and we ordered.

It was time to open gifts. We both pulled presents out from our bags at the same moment. We exchanged across the table, careful not to knock over our drinks, looked at each other, smiled and started unwrapping at exactly the same time. I heard Sam exclaim, and start laughing. I'd given her one of those wooden frames that held three pictures: Marty and Mickey, who were together as December in the calendar, one of all of us on the back of the fire engine in Chico that the driver had taken right before the picnic, and one of she and I overlooking the harbor in Trinidad. I'd had the bottom engraved with *Sam and Natalie's Most Excellent Adventure: forever etched in memory.* She thanked me and said she couldn't wait to hang it up— wherever she lived next.

This just started more tears as I thought about her being gone, but I continued on, opening my gift from Sam. It was a framed, matted photo of Hammer and I in the Spyder, the day I'd taken him for the drive. She had written, *Wuv, twu wuv* at the bottom on the matting in silver sparkly ink. Leave it to Sam to put a Princess Bride reference on the frame. I loved it! "I didn't know you were there that day!"

"We mortals too have our secrets," was her reply, and then she added how that's the reason she seemed impatient that day, because after I'd dropped her off, she must have hurried to my gym to snap this shot, and had been waiting for me to gather my courage.

"It's all so clear to me now," I said, laughing and crying at the same time. I thanked her, saying I couldn't wait to hang it up, on the wall where I was now living—until further notice.

We finished our dinner and strolled around outside. It was freezing but we both had scarves, hats, and gloves on. "I can't believe Christmas is only a week away."

"I know," Sam agreed. "It's been quite a year."

"Sure has," I said sighing. "I'm glad it happened, and I'm glad it's nearly over."

"Me too! Have you heard from Hammer lately?"

"Yes, a few days ago he left a message saying he expected to be home on Christmas Eve."

"Oh boy. That doesn't leave you much time together."

"Not really. He wants to do Christmas Eve with his parents, and Christmas with me, which works for me."

We parted ways at her car, and I walked to mine, drove home, and prepared to finish Christmas shopping the next day. I never wanted to be a last minute shopper, because it meant putting up with horrendous crowds and I was more an in-and-out type of girl. This year, finances made it necessary to shop the week before Christmas, and since I worked mornings at the coffee shop I'd have to do it later in the day. I had to get a good night's sleep, so I crawled into bed almost immediately, putting my pillow over my head to regulate my breathing. What do you know? My body actually fell for it.

The next morning, I counted my tips during break. $40. Not bad for two and a half hours. People must be in the Christmas spirit. It'd sure been a busy morning. I'd sold a ton of peppermint mochas. They also wanted gingerbread lattes, but I told them that was a Starbucks specialty drink, and suggested a peppermint or toasted marshmallow mocha. I looked forward to getting off work and hitting the stores, because I still hadn't found the perfect gift for my trainer, and I had a couple special places to look for what I had in mind for Hammer.

I saw out the front window of the coffee stand a familiar vehicle turn off the roadway toward the stand. It was Cameron and Courtney in their parents' car! Oh Lord. Now was the first and only time I wished for a co-worker who could cover for me.

They pulled up to the window. "Hi," said the new nanny, who I recognized from my visit. I prayed she wouldn't open the back window, but I could already hear them shouting my name.

"Hi! How are you?"

"Well, I'm doing alright, but they kept asking if we could visit the Lollipop Man. They've asked me for two weeks, and finally today we were driving by and I figured out from their shrieks of delight that this was the Lollipop Stand... And you must be Natalie."

"Yep, that's me. I'm the new Lollipop Lady," I said, trying to keep the conversation light.

"Sara," she said, somewhat coolly. I figured it was a safe bet to assume the kids were driving her nuts.

I heard them asking, and saw her lurch as Cameron kicked her seat, so she opened the back window. "Hi Natalie!" They said in unison. "How come you not come back?" Cameron asked.

Ooh. Natalie, think fast. "Well Cam, I didn't have much of a choice. See, I know Santa Claus, who needed extra help this Christmas because his elves were overworked. He gave me a call asking if I was available, so I said yes, I could help out by making coffee for the Clauses and the elves and reindeer."

"Wow! You work for Santa Claus?"

"Indirectly, yes. But please keep it a secret, I'm not supposed to tell." By this point, Cameron and Courtney were wide-eyed, and even Sara was chuckling. "He gave me something to give to you. First I'll make your drinks and then I'll go and get your gifts." Cameron repeated to his sister what I said, even though I was sure she could hear me too, all the way on the other side of the back seat.

Sara ordered a tall soy vanilla latte and two small hot chocolates. Cam asked for a lollipop, and I told him we had something even better, and handed Sara three candy canes—a big one for her, and two little ones for the kids. They didn't need a massive sugar high today, I could tell.

"So what're you doing today? Gonna go do something fun?" I asked.

"Yeah, we're probably going to the park. It just seems to be that kind of a day," she said.

"I hear you," I said. They needed to run around and release that energy. "Looks like a nice dry day for it."

"Yeah, those are hard to come by around here. I'm from eastern Oregon," she said.

"Ah. Well, the summer makes it worth it to live here, some say. I tend to agree, although I wouldn't mind more blue sky." I finished making the drinks and handed them over. "Maybe, Cam, Sara can show you later how to stir your hot chocolate with your candy cane. It makes a yummy taste and it's neat to see the candy cane disappear."

"Good idea," Sara said.

I checked the front window and there were no other customers. "Give me a sec go to my car. It's that one," I said, pointing so Sara could pull up next to it. She did, and I got out two stuffed animals for the kids: a giraffe for Cameron and a horse for Courtney. "They both talk if you squeeze them."

"A horse is a horse, of course, of course," sang Courtney's, and continued with the song from Mr. Ed. I saw that they were showing reruns of it, so I hoped she would know the song. Sure enough, she sang along with it.

"What does a mother giraffe say to her baby after its bath?" the giraffe asked. "I think you missed a spot." It went on and on telling corny giraffe jokes in a voice similar to Mr. Ed's. I'm sure Sara would want to ring my neck before long for giving them talking toys, but I was really hoping they'd play with them for a while later so she could catch a break.

"Why don't we put those up in front with Sara, and you can play with them later?" I suggested, taking them too quickly for protests. "They're special toys from Santa and can't get dirty."

"Thanks, Natalie," Sara said, closing the back windows. I waved goodbye to the kids. "Can I have a word?"

"Sure," I said. Luckily, we seemed to be having a lull at work.

She hopped out and closed the door. "I was just wondering, well, what happened, why you did leave? The parents never told me."

"Oh. Well, how long have you been in Washington?"

"About a year."

"In this area?"

"Yeah."

"Did you happen to see the photo in the paper of me and the kids?"

"On Halloween, with the fire at the theater? Oh my God, that was you!"

"Yeah, that was me. Well, they didn't like that so much, their kids being on the front page. They fired me because I took their kids to the fire, which was because they had told me they were going to the movies and I thought they might be there."

"I see. Thanks for telling me."

"No problem. It's not a secret," I said, smiling. "What happened was too public, and this is too small a town for that."

"No kidding. Can I ask you one more thing?"

"Shoot."

"Did the kids ever stop testing you?"

"No." I thought for a minute of any advice I could give her. "Just be consistent. You already have more respect than their parents, because they either punish the kids or cater to their every whim, and you, I'm sure, are more firm and less...well, gushy."

"That's for sure. Gushy gooey I am not."

"Good. Keep it up and eventually they'll find new tests. At least that part never gets boring."

She laughed, and asked if I would go to coffee with her sometime. I agreed and gave her my cell number. I knew how nice it would have been to have someone show me the ropes, so I would have had a clue about these particular alien kids.

They drove off, waving, and I went and finished my shift, smiling at how funny life could be sometimes.

With Christmas a day away, the world was abuzz with a mix of cheer and stress. Pretty much that meant 95% were stressed, the other 5% put on happy faces. I was amazed that a large portion of the western world repeated this process every year, with increasing chaos, and that somehow, some way, we got through it. The day after Thanksgiving, one year, people had been trampled over when the department store opened. The news had a clip of it they kept repeating where this woman fell and her wig came off, and people just kept rushing by. It would've been great to see someone helping her up, but in the clip, played and rewound on the news over and over, no one did.

I wasn't playing that clip in my mind as I went shopping though. All I felt was peace, even with all the humanity scrambling around me. I guess I was reserving my frenetic energy for later. It was best spent on workouts, I had discovered, or in an emergency. The true meaning of Christmas was not supposed to be chaos, but calm. Unfortunately, most people had to go through the chaos to get there, and then the calm didn't last.

I wondered what Christmas would be like with Cameron and Courtney. Probably not calm, but hopefully filled with a lot of love and happiness. Same with the family across the street. I would miss my charges, but at least Sara had brought them by.

My cell phone rang a few times while I was shopping but there was so much noise I couldn't have heard the person other end anyway, so I turned it off and focused on gift finding.

I found my trainer's gift right away. It was a beautiful framed silver plate, which had a black symbol on it, etched in black. It was the Chinese symbol for long life, and the piece had been designed to be a wall hanging. It was a set, but I only purchased him that one symbol for starters. I still had Hammer's gift to take care of.

Hammer was not easy to shop for, because his current lifestyle didn't really allow for a lot of toys. He wasn't into video games, didn't watch a ton of television—just another reason, of many, to love him. And I did. I really did. I had missed Hammer a lot while he'd been gone, and was so looking forward to spending Christmas together.

Then I thought of the perfect thing. I would have to go to the city to get it, but I didn't care. I drove to the ferry, and actually drove on instead of walking even though it was more expensive. The gift I was thinking of, I wouldn't be able to carry easily.

This will be great, I thought. I'd stop by Krispy Kreme too, since there weren't any on my side of the water yet, and get some doughnuts for my oddball cat who spoke to me only in dreams.

I usually stayed in my car while riding the ferry, but today I wanted to blend in to the sea of faces. I made my way upstairs, enjoying the breeze for a moment and then going inside to sit down. It was very crowded, so I considered myself lucky to find a spot as I looked out the window of the ferry, thoughts quickly turning to being with Hammer again. It was like a dream, when we were together, like time out of time.

Suddenly, I heard my name being shouted. So much for being invisible.

Cameron and Courtney ran towards me, each picking a knee, and clamping on. They stood in front of me, jumping up and down on my toes, but I didn't mind—I had on thick boots to keep my feet warm. The kids were all dressed up in cute matching winter outfits; Cameron's was blue, and Courtney's pink. Surely a grandparent thing—wanting to keep them tiny as long as possible.

Sara came sidling up behind them, out of breath from chasing them. "You don't by chance happen to have a spare leash in your bag, do you?" she said, laughing.

I chuckled. "No, but I hear with those wooden mops they use on the ferry to clean up spills, you can just take off the mop part, wrap a small bungee cord around each kid, loop it around and hoist it onto your back. That way, you can still see both of them, and you may take out a few pedestrians, walking around Seattle, but it'd be their fault for invading your space bubble anyway."

She laughed and I could tell she was in need of a sanity break. The kids wondered what we were laughing at, so I asked them what they were going to do in Seattle.

"We go to arcade! Big, big one!" Cameron said, delighted, stretching his arms out to simulate the length of the arcade. I knew the one he was talking about. It had several floors and was really hopping.

"Yah!" Courtney chimed in, throwing an arm in the air and jumping up and down like the little cheerleader she was destined to be someday.

"Sounds like fun, guys!"

"I'm sure it'll be interesting," Sara said.

"Whose idea was it?"

"Their parents suggested it," she said.

"Hmm," I said, smiling and looking out the window to hide what I was thinking. I was wondering what the hell the parents were thinking, having the new nanny take their kids to a place where keeping them under control would put her to the test. She would need someone to help her harness these kids, with older kids running all over the place. It was a great place to go, for older kids, or maybe even for younger kids, who had one parent or guardian per kid. I mean, maybe the carousel, or the aquarium, but suggesting bringing toddlers to the arcade? With one nanny?!?!

I could feel myself starting to get upset. How much did these parents truly care about these tiny little lives? The possibility of them getting hurt was big, and I didn't want to chance it. Here I was, not getting paid anymore for watching them, and still having the fierce desire to protect them. My hands curled into fists, my fingernails digging into my palms. I knew I had to be alone, so I excused myself and said I needed to go to the bathroom.

Once I rounded the corner, out of sight of Sara, the kids and everyone else, I closed my eyes and reappeared upstairs, on the upper most deck, back in the crisp cold wind. I stood for a second, letting it penetrate me to the core, wanting the uneasy feeling in my gut to go away. Unfortunately, it was still there.

I whipped along the perimeter of the deck. I didn't even care today if anyone had seen me appear out of nowhere—I was livid. Apparently, the parents hadn't heard me or learned from my message at all. They hadn't heard a word I'd said about the safety of their children or about how they would just suddenly get the urge and run in opposite directions. I tried counting to ten, but it didn't work. I tried counting backwards from ten. That didn't work either. My fingers gripped the railing tight and I closed my eyes.

"Natalie."

Hearing the familiar voice behind me, I opened my eyes and gazed out at the water. I smiled as I realized who it was.

"It's been quite a year for you, hasn't it?"

I turned around. "It sure has," I said, shaking my head, looking into the dark, shining eyes of Vin Diesel.

"I'm here to offer advice, if you want it," he said.

"Not only do I want it, I need it."

"Well, you can't do much about what those parents do or how much they care about their kids."

"That's true, I can't."

"What do you have the power to change, then?"

"I don't know. I can't think, in this case, what I am supposed to do. I only know I'm supposed to use my power to the highest good. But I don't see how disappearing and reappearing could work for me today."

"You don't, huh?"

"Not really. I mean, the only thing I know I can do is to avert disaster by grabbing a kid and getting out of harm's way. I'm not sure what else I'm set up to do. This superhero thing is new to me and I guess that's why I called in reinforcements."

"Meaning me."

"In a word, yes."

"You know, Natalie, I'm kind of a straight-to-the-point kind of guy."

"I can see that about you."

"That means I'm not going to make you work for it. I'm just going to spill it. I may get in trouble for this later," he said, looking up, "but it's a small price to pay for offering you some relief."

"I appreciate that. Can I ask you something first?"

"But of course," he said, flashing that famous grin.

"How much of my life have you seen? I mean, do you have a rough idea of what's happened or the whole sordid story?"

"The whole, sordid story," he said, smiling.

"You know my teacher and Jade?"

"Yes. Whatever is important to you, is also important for us, your guardians and advisors, to see."

"Gotcha. Well then that's a relief. I don't have to be embarrassed, because you already know everything."

"Yeah. And those boudoir scenes, phew!" he said, wiping his forehead.

I laughed. Nothing like a little humor to lighten the mood around here.

"Seriously though, what I'm here to tell you is, you can hold off on the being invisible part. It's for bigger purposes than getting out of a pickle or avoiding your morning commute."

"Good to know," I said.

"I don't know if you're aware of this, Natalie, but you have an amazing power to convince and to change things without using any supernatural superhuman skill."

"No, I didn't, but I'll consider that. Anything else you can tell me? Hints, tips, tasty tidbits?"

"Just one. Breathe. Breathe deeply, and when you get home tonight, don't just dive into the shower or bathtub. Put your feet up for twenty minutes first. It'll help you relax and shake off the day."

"Thanks, Vin," I said, wondering what that meant the day would hold. Sheesh.

"No problem." He started to turn and walk away, didn't just vanish into thin air. Because of this, I had an extra second to think.

I don't know what came over me. Well, actually I do. I had been through a lot of these scenarios, and was getting the idea that they were mine and no one else's. That meant I could do whatever the heck I wanted. What came over me was pure, unadulterated desire of the first degree.

"Vin, wait." He turned around, and before he had the chance to stop me, I grabbed the front of his shirt, and pulled him in for a nice, long kiss. It was wet, wild, and totally worth it.

I released him. "How's that for to-the-point?" I said. I didn't know where this new confidence was coming from, but it felt mighty good. He gave me a hug and a high five, said "That…was *awesome*. Peace out, Ninja Nanny," we smiled at each other, and then we both disappeared.

I don't know where Vin reappeared. Probably somewhere in California. Or maybe Bora Bora. I don't know why I didn't choose George Clooney either, but maybe he was busy learning lines or taking care of his pig. It didn't matter. Vin Diesel it was, and at that point I wouldn't have accepted advice from anyone else.

If I was a nanny of the villainous sort, and because life had been so challenging lately, I might have asked Vin to take me with him, but unfortunately I couldn't be selfish when I had kids to protect. So unlike him, I reappeared inside a bathroom stall. Luckily, I chose an empty one.

Taking a moment to compose myself, I walked out of the stall, washed my hands as if I'd used it, and back to the kids and Sara. "Can I talk to you for a minute?" I asked her.

"Sure," she said, and we went over where we could still see the kids, who for a rare moment were mesmerized doing nothing but looking out the window. Sara must have hypnotized them.

"How would you like some company today? We could have that coffee we talked about, even if it's a struggle to keep the kids still."

"Sure!" she said, brightening. "I could use the extra hand." She thought for a second. "Well, unless you had other plans. I wouldn't want to interrupt."

"Just picking up a few last minute Christmas gifts. Did you guys walk onboard?"

"We did."

"Great. I drove, so I can take us to the arcade, if that's really where you want to go."

"Well actually I don't, but I'm afraid since the parents already told the kids we're going there…"

"We're stuck." I could just imagine one of the parents getting this brilliant brain flash in the middle of the night, deciding it and springing it on the new nanny right in front of the kids, and Sara having just walked in, not had any coffee yet, agreeing to it while still half asleep.

"Yeah. They'd be terribly disappointed."

"And you wouldn't want this to get back to Mom and Dad."

"Not really. Or hear about it for the rest of my natural born life."

"No kidding."

We walked back over to the kids, each grabbed one since the ferry was about to dock and headed down to my rig. It didn't have car seats, which Cameron made a big deal out of, but it wasn't like I was going on the freeway, only up the hill a few blocks and then parking, so I strapped them in and we were off. Somehow, I felt safer with them in my car and my care than thinking of Sara walking them up by herself, through hordes of strangers. I knew he would forget to tell his parents about the car seats after having the time of his life in Seattle.

I drove back onto the ferry after a long, exhausting day of fun with kids. As I watched Sara take them upstairs, I really didn't know if I could handle having my own, even though I heard it was easier if I didn't inherit two, all at once, already in their toddler years. I wasn't sure I believed that.

The arcade visit was less of a challenge with two of us watching for Cameron's sudden dashing and darting all over the place. He pulled quite a few of those little tricks, but either Sara or I caught him, every time. We only spent a few minutes there before the kids realized they were too young for a lot of the games, and then went on the carousel at Westlake Center and had a great time. Maybe nannies should come in pairs. The kids had been kept safe without any superhero stuff, just like Vin had said. I knew I should use my powers sparingly for now, because I still wasn't sure what all they were, or how I would find out.

Right now, there was Christmas to contend with. It was Christmas Eve and I didn't even know if my boyfriend would make it home. Remembering to check my messages paid off. Hammer would be home on Christmas, to spend it with me. I couldn't have been more thrilled. I missed him so much. Unfortunately, because of the impromptu trip to Seattle, I didn't have a chance to buy his Christmas present, not to mention the Krispy Kremes for Kiki. I would get online after I got home to take care of the latter. Normally I'd be upset and worry myself into a tizzy about what I was going to do, but tonight I just wanted to relax, take Vin's advice, put my feet up, and then kick back in the tub.

When I got home, there was a huge box at the door. I mean this box came up to my waist and it was fully wrapped in blue and gold paper with gold ribbon curled up on top. The size of the thing reminded me of the movie Serendipity when John Corbett's character asked Kate Beckinsale's character to marry him, and there was a huge box that housed a bunch of smaller boxes and inside the smallest one was a ring. Was this the same? I doubted Hammer would steal a proposal idea from a movie. Was he home early? I looked around, and didn't see Hammer or anyone spying on me, so I took the box inside. I couldn't stop staring at it as I took my coat off and absently said hello to Kiki.

I didn't hear any ticking, so I didn't think it was a bomb. What could it be? Was there a kid in here? Would this be like in Ally McBeal when she had a daughter show up because she had donated an egg umpteen years ago and forgotten about it? If so, I would probably do what she did and faint right there on the spot.

I didn't see any note saying not to open this until Christmas, but there was a card on top, which was also enormous for a card. On the front, Santa was grabbing a cookie while making sure he wasn't being spied on. I opened it. In handwriting that didn't belong to Hammer, it said "This is our gift to you, Natalie, for all you've done and all the laughs you've given us this year. We really appreciated the cookies you brought, and thought you could use something to cuddle up with on the nights Hammer is out of town. Plus, everyone should open a present on Christmas Eve. With love, your favorite firefighters." I was pretty sure Tim had written the card.

I felt myself getting emotional. Those guys were just too sweet. Then something came over me—must've been that pesky curiosity. It just took over. Did they buy me a body pillow? A huge stuffed animal? A Spongebob, a Tweety Bird? An Ewok, perhaps?

I didn't know, so I ripped it open.

It was not a box of boxes or an Ewok. Inside was a giant animal carrier. "Oh my God!" I said. I peered inside. It was a little calico kitten. "Well hello there, cutie," I said. "You must've been cold waiting outside for as long as you did." But the kitten actually looked pretty comfortable, as it was snuggled into a bunch of blankets and it looked like it'd recently woken up. Kiki sidled up to the crate, and stuck her green eye up to one of the holes like she was peering through too. "What do you think, Ki? A little friend for you for Christmas?"

Kiki just stared at me, one blue eye and one green. She looked like someone had slapped her behind. I'm sure she was wondering if I'd forgone the Krispy Kremes in lieu of the kitten. I decided to let her think I had, for now... I would order the real thing and make it up to her, but the bakery in town had amazing pastries so I could go there in the next few days to take care of the feline sweet tooth. Christmas was special, no matter who was present.

I let the kitten out and checked to see the gender, but it was too early to tell. Usually Calico cats were girls, but I had seen a boy once. I set about building a fire, pretending not to watch while Kiki and the new one sniffed each other. Kiki was never aggressive toward other cats, but she did like her space. I knew I'd be able to tell within a few minutes if they would be compatible, or just tolerate each other or pretend the other one didn't exist. "You know, Kiki, this will go a lot more smoothly if you show the new guy around, give him a tour of his new home." I checked for a reaction, and Kiki seemed to be mulling it over, looking up at the ceiling, one corner of her mouth higher than the other. I was still trying to trick her into talking, but didn't want to demand an answer, because then she'd figure it out. I waited. And while I waited, I unpacked the rest of the carrier.

Those guys had thought of everything—toys, catnip, kitten food, and a little dish with "Claw" written on the side. I started to cry. I couldn't help it. I had never met a group of people so thoughtful in my life. I unpacked it and put the carrier in the closet, getting out the stockings I'd bought for Hammer and Kiki, making sure everything was in there, and putting them on the mantle.

When I turned around, both felines had left the room. I figured maybe Kiki had taken my advice, so I continued getting ready for tomorrow. I wanted to make Hammer a good meal, so after checking that I had the necessary ingredients, I turned on the bath water. I knew exactly what my plan was, since I hadn't gotten his present yet. I was going to give myself to him for Christmas.

After my bath, I crawled onto the couch in my robe. Underneath, I wore the lingerie that I hadn't gotten to show him because of the movie theater fire. It was a white lace teddy with garter belts and thigh highs. I was hoping he'd come over first thing in the morning, so we could spend the morning opening presents and then go directly to bed. I needed that man's arms around me in the worst way.

It was so comfortable there, by the fire, and I just relaxed, with a couple pillows under my head and my feet elevated on the end of the couch. I thought for a moment about what a day it had been, and laughed to myself. I just let it fade away. Soon, I'd be able to let the year fade away, and hot diggety dog was I ecstatic about that. I let out a deep sigh, and looked at the place, pleased with myself. I had a mini living tree that was being planted outside after Christmas. The lights twinkled, the tinsel shined, and Kiki meowed.

She was sitting by the fire with her front leg, which looked like an arm, around the kitten's back, and they were both looking at me. "Happy, Keekster?"

"Sure ammmmeow," she said.

"What should we name your new friend?" I asked.

"Hmmm....well, I thought I'd let you know that it's a boy," Kiki said.

"Good! A younger man for you."

Kiki did what I can only describe as a cat's laugh, and said, "I think his nammme should be Claw, like on the bowl," she said. "It fits my bad girl image to have a younger boyfriend named Claw."

"As you wish. Claw it is, then." I said. "Welcome to the family, little dude." I almost couldn't believe it, but they high 5'd each other. He was a quick learner, this Claw. I laughed, and Kiki cleared her throat.

"Natalie?"

"Yes?"

"I think Christmas should be spelled with a K."

It was at that point that my own laughter woke me up. Oddly enough, Kiki and Claw were sitting side by side next to the fire in exactly the same spot as in my dream. They were quiet for the rest of the night, no speaking, and finally drifted off to sleep so I could play Santa and put presents under the tree. I had the one for my Sifu, for Jade, one for Hammer's parents who I still hadn't met, one for Tim, one for my boss at the coffee stand, and some extra special cans of more expensive tuna for Kiki, and now for Claw to share. Finished, I stood with my arms folded and surveyed my work, when something outside caught my eye.

It was snowing. How perfect—the first snow of the season on Christmas Eve. I hoped Hammer would be all right.

I sat back down on the couch. It was only 8:30pm, but my eyelids were heavy and I thought it wouldn't be such a bad thing if I drifted off right there. Then I heard something I hadn't heard in years, or maybe since my childhood imagination.

…Sleigh bells?…

I got up, looked out the window. *Unbelievable.*

"Ho ho ho!" I heard, booming across the rooftops. "Ho ho ho! Merry Christmas! Merrrrrry Christmas!"

I had to see where that was coming from. I looked up in the sky, and didn't see any reindeer attached to a sleigh. "That's it," I said to myself. If Santa, Rudolph and company come around the corner, I'm committing myself." I heard a siren. I pulled my robe tight and opened the door.

The siren got closer and closer, and still closer. What the bleep? I thought. No smoke could be smelled, I saw no fires. All of a sudden, a fire engine came around the corner of my apartment complex.

There was a red painted sleigh on top with white lights all the way around the frame, and a Santa. He was ringing sleigh bells, and yelling "Merry Christmas." The siren was off now, and they parked right in front of my apartment.

Santa got down from the sleigh, and Tim waved at me from the driver's seat of the truck. I waved back, smiling and watching as Santa, with a huge belly that shook like jelly but sounded like crumpled up newspaper, came to my door, heavy boots trampling through the freshly falling snow.

It was Hammer, dressed up in a Santa suit. "Ho Ho Ho! Merry Christmas! Got a kiss for Santa?" he said, grinning under his beard.

"Oh my God, what are you doing here?" I asked, as he smothered my mouth with the beard. I hugged him hard enough to squeeze some of the stuffing out of his stomach. "Sorry Santa, I got a little carried away," I said.

"Ho ho ho…no problem, little lady," winking.

"Didn't you spend tonight with your parents?" I asked.

"Yep. We already opened gifts and everything. Then the guy who was supposed to play Santa canceled, and guess who got stuck doing it. I jabbed his stomach, and he said "Yep, yours truly. But I don't mind. Seeing the looks on the kids' faces just melts my heart," he said.

"I know what you mean." I was pretty much stunned speechless by this point, to have Hammer standing here in a Santa suit. Then I saw that Tim was still sitting out in the truck. "Hammer, can we invite Tim inside? He doesn't need to sit out there alone."

"Well actually, yes. I was hoping he could use your bathroom to change into the Santa outfit, because there's an hour left before we're done and I want to stay here if it's okay with you."

"If it's okay? Of course it's okay. I've missed you so much these past weeks."

"Me too. *So* much." I hugged him again, just thrilled to have him back, and went to open the door and motion Tim inside. "Hold on a sec. I have to talk to you," he said, a seriousness coming over his face that I had never seen before.

He shut the door, took my hands. "Natalie." He said, looking deeply into my eyes and clearing his throat. He knelt down in front of me. I could feel his hands shaking as they held mine, tightly. "I love you. I loved you the first minute I saw you, and every minute together since has filled my heart with more love, because I have gotten to know you in depth, Natalie, and I absolutely adore what's there. I missed the heck out of my badass girlfriend." I smiled, touching his hair. Honestly, I was probably more like grinning from ear to ear now.

"I can't imagine life without you. I love you so much." He took a deep breath, and looked into my face, studying it intensely. "Will you marry me?"

I looked down at him, that handsome face with those big blue eyes looking deep into my soul, and my tears started to flow. "Hammer, I love you right back. I have no idea what the future holds for me, but I want you to be part of it," I said. "Yes, I will marry you. Yes. YES!"

He picked me up and spun me around. We were both crying out of happiness now. My robe came partially undone, and he saw what was underneath. "Whoa."

"Um yeah." I said, feeling shy all of a sudden. "Circumstances prevented me from getting your gift on time, so I was going to be your Christmas present, and I wrapped myself up in this."

"Yum," he said. "Well then, we better get Tim in here and out of here so we can get to the business of unwrapping."

We held each other for a moment, and kissed, and looked out the window, holding each other, wanting to hold onto the moment. There was Tim, standing in the snow beside the fire engine, crying. He gave the thumbs up sign, and Hammer returned it. He motioned Tim over and opened the door. Tim bounded right in and gave Hammer a great big bear hug, and then hugged me, a little more gently.

"Congratulations, you two," he said.

I thanked him, and Hammer did too. Hammer mumbled something about going out to get a change of clothes from the truck, and ran outside.

"Tim, was that your handwriting on my Christmas card?"

A slow blush spread across his cheeks. "Yes, it was."

"Was it your idea to get me a kitten?"

"Hammer and I cooked that one up together on the phone, couple weeks back," he said. I knew Tim was being modest and it'd been his initial idea, so I took his arm, and sat him down on the couch, thanked him, and told him it touched me deeply. I gave him his Christmas present that was under the tree. "You're quite a gal, Natalie," he said, eyes watery.

My heart was full to the point of overflowing with love and joy and total excitement, and after I went to make the guys some cider, Hammer came back in with his overnight bag. They talked in hushed voices for a moment until I came back out with the cider, and then all talking ceased.

"What's going on, guys?" I asked, smiling.

"Nothing at all," Hammer said, his lips in a secret smile. He headed off to the bathroom, and came out two minutes later as himself. "All yours, Tim," he said, pointing the way.

Hammer sat down on the couch and I poured him some spiced cider. He didn't drink cider that often, but it was cold outside and he wasn't picky. He had just become engaged. I wasn't sure if there was a ring, or if he wanted to pick that out together, but I figured it if he had bought it, it might come out tomorrow morning on Christmas, and that was fine with me.

For tonight, I just wanted him all to myself, and that was more than enough.

Hammer was in the shower. I was waiting for him to finish so we could open presents, or actually so that I could open mine. He had unwrapped his present quite well last night.

The cats were still asleep in Kiki's bed, and I started breakfast. I enjoyed the smell of coffee brewing. Hammer was a pure, unadulterated coffee man—no peppermint mochas or gingerbread lattes or spiced cider for him. He liked it with a splash of milk and no sugar. I poured him a big mug of it, put it on the counter, and set about making the world's best firefighter breakfast ever: scrambled eggs with avocado, hashed browns and cut up sausage and chicken, all rolled into a warmed burrito—enough protein and carbs to feed a small army, all going into Hammer's 6-pack. Well actually he had more of an 8-pack, but I didn't mind a bit.

I could never eat immediately after waking, so I downed some coffee and dove into the shower while he ate, and then it was time to open presents. ☺

We let Kiki open her stocking first. I'd gotten her a bunch of toys, catnip, and a gift certificate for the pet store. She shared with Claw, who was thrilled with just his own toys and having a new home. I found something under the tree for Kiki and handed it over. Would she unwrap it herself or pretend like she didn't know how?

My gifted feline attacked the curling ribbon on top of the package, and while doing that, managed to rip the wrapping paper to shreds, thereby unwrapping her gift. Hammer and I watched in amazement as she did this in a matter of seconds, and then pounced on the box and looked up at me expectantly. "If you'll just remove yourself from the box, I'll open it for you," I said. She hopped right off, and I noticed

Hammer give her this look, like he knew that she knew exactly what we said.

"This is what I'm saying," I said, by way of explanation. She rubbed back and forth on my back while I did this, showing me some love, and I lifted up top of the box, popped open a can of tuna and gave it to her. "Sorry it's not what you asked for, Kiki, but I ordered some donuts online and they should arrive before too long."

Hammer laughed as I opened the tuna with the can opener I'd also put in the box, and Kiki inhaled the tuna and looked at me for more. "Kiki, I hope you appreciate your mom's kindness."

She didn't reply, just gave him a look that seemed to say "You're *so* beneath me."

Claw came up and kissed my nose with his, and looked at my hand, licking his chops. I gave him some too. With all the tuna and catnip toys, they'd be taking some coma-like naps later. I poured some milk into their dishes, and Hammer asked what my plans were for New Year's Eve. I looked at him for a moment, and said, "Actually, I haven't made any. I was hoping we could spend it together. Will you be here?"

"No."

"Oh. Really? Where are you going?"

"One sec." He got up and took his jacket off the hook, brought it over with him and sat down, smiling.

"Are you cold?"

"Nope," he said, still smiling.

"What's up with that grin?" I asked, starting to grin too. Hammer's grin was infectious.

He reached into his pocket and pulled out an envelope. "Merry Christmas, Natalie," he said. He handed me the envelope. "There's a ring, too, but I'm waiting for the right moment." I was speechless at that last part. I took the envelope, wondering what this could possibly be.

I slid my fingers inside, feeling tickets. Tickets to what? To where? A concert for New Year's? A play? A Mariners game? A movie? A trip for two to Vegas? I could not believe my eyes when I looked at what I was holding in my hand: Two tickets to San Francisco International Airport. "We're going to California?"

He just smiled at me, gauging my reaction.

"I've never been to San Francisco."

"I know, and you've always wanted to, but we're not just going to San Francisco."

All of a sudden, I realized where we were going. "Oh my God. You're taking me to Half Moon Bay." I looked up at him and he was already blurry though the sudden tears in my eyes, but I saw him nodding.

"How did you know?"

"I called Sam asking for suggestions. Looked her up in the phone book—Dex is a useful tool."

I laughed, loving every thought this man had ever had, and tackled him to the ground with a hug and kisses. I kissed him like a million times. "You just scored *mega*points," I said through the kisses.

After I made sure to cover all my bases, I composed myself and looked more carefully at the tickets. They were for December 26—the following night! I looked up at him.

"Yes, I checked the temperatures there—highs of 67-70 degrees all week—global warming is cooperating, and yeah, we have a lot to do," he said, reading my mind. "We have to see my parents, pack our bags…"

"Arrange for a kitty sitter—"

"Already done," he said. "Sam."

"Really? I mean really?" Luckily, she was still here and hadn't moved to California with Marty yet. I was astonished by how well Hammer had thought this through. "Well, I do have to work a couple days between now and New Year's."

"No you don't," he said, grinning again.

"*What?*"

"I sort of had Tim talk to your boss. We were all in cahoots."

"You are some piece of work." I could say no more. He had thought of everything. "What can I do to help? Do we need to arrange a taxi ride to the airport?"

"The ride is taken care of. You just pack a bag or two and we'll head over to my parents' house so you can finally meet each other. And tomorrow you can de-stress, and you'll have a whole week to relax and unwind. We can do as much or as little as you like on this trip."

I had never had anyone do anything like this for me, and it floored me. I'd always done everything for myself. I was an independent woman of action. Today, I just sat there, looking out at the snow for a minute, and thought. I thought about my life, my plan, my path. The Way. I knew that whatever happened, I wanted Hammer by my side. We were meant to be together and I couldn't ever see that changing. I thought about the firefighter signs and the fact that they'd likely, and thankfully, cease now that I had come full circle into Hammer's arms. Our vacation wouldn't be like the road trip. It'd be a trip the likes of which I'd never experienced.

Half Moon Bay

Hammer had already packed. The bag he'd brought in last night was actually for the trip, clever man. So he played with the cats outside, showing Claw what snow felt like as it was his first experience with it. I watched for a minute and went to the bedroom to do my own packing.

I finished in about 20 minutes, and stretched across the bed, taking a little rest before we headed out. I could hear Hammer outside, doing what sounded like a snow angel, and laughed at the thought of him teaching that to Kiki and Claw.

All of a sudden, it felt like I was being sucked into a giant vacuum. I stood, facing my trainer and Jade in the garden of the sanctuary. "Wow, this is unexpected," I said, gaining my land legs again after being funneled through a time warp.

"Natalie, we wanted to talk to you before you left on the trip, so that we wouldn't have to bother you during," Jade said.

"Congratulations," Jin said, smiling.

"Thank you. I wish I would've known so I could've brought you your gifts."

"We can get them later, it's fine. Thank you." I didn't know if Jin and Jade celebrated Christmas, but they were surrounded by it in our culture so I thought it only appropriate as a symbol of gratitude for all they'd done for me. I knew I wouldn't be staying in California long, so I wasn't worried. California was for vacationing, but Washington was home.

"We summoned you here so we could tell you something very important. Let's sit."

We sat, had tea and talked. Jade told me I was meant for more, more than I gave myself credit for—more than a wife, more than a barista. I was happy with those titles, but she said I had so much yet to learn, if I wished.

They told me about the history of Ninjitsu. It took centuries to become a deadly art form. Before that, mountain dwellers on the largest of the Japanese islands created it, roughly 1100 years ago. They believed that all parts of nature were an extension of themselves, so were very connected to the earth. They got energy, strength and stamina from the earth and would, along with using secret words and the power of intention, use nature itself to focus. They stood under icy waterfalls, hung over cliffs and walked through fire to conquer fear. These same challenges would be available to me if I wanted to advance.

My Sifu said that the Ninja were mainly farmers and that they only studied as a means of self-defense. That part I knew. I was never to use my skills with the intent to harm anyone, and I never had. After the fall of the T'ang Dynasty in China when many exiled soldiers, academics and military escaped to Japan to avoid retribution, the Ninja farmer families were exposed to their beliefs and strategies, creating what became Ninjitsu.

There were around 80 clans during the height of Ninjitsu, and they used their resources to protect their own members. Unfortunately, the original intent of these people was polluted when Japan's government considered them a threat, and rumor spread about their powers. At the same time, traitors would contract for spying and killing, and regrettably, they became the stereotype assassin Ninja we know in popular culture. The whole thing got out of control.

Sifu Jin told me Ninjitsu is the art of stealth. He would teach me to throw the Ninja star, a weapon of stealth that could be easily hidden. But more importantly, he would teach me to be silent and surreptitious in my movements. We would go out into nature, practice, and perfect, so I could protect.

I sat there for a moment, taking it all in.

"You can think about it," he said. "While you think, we will prepare the practices and tests for you, should you choose to take this on. And we have a gift for you."

Jade bowed before me, presenting me with a Ninja star in a black velvet case. It was beautiful—made of hard carbon steel that shined in the sun. "Ninja Nanny, this is your symbol to take with you wherever you can, reminding you of who you are and your true purpose, which as you know is to keep children safe."

Still in shock, I accepted the gift, and thanked them. I bowed to both of them individually. We spoke for a few more minutes, and then it was time for me to go.

"We will talk soon," Jin said. "Now go, and enjoy your vacation."

"Thank you both," I said, walking away and then turning back. "Jin?"

"Yes, Phoenix?"

"When I fought the ninja, I don't know what happened, but... I wasn't there. I didn't deserve the congratulations you gave me."

"What do you mean?"

"I went back in time. To a boys' martial arts camp, in Japan... I was five."

"Yes?" he prompted, a smile playing at the corners of his mouth.

"All the kids were sparring, and you were there. It was easy to see you. You looked directly at me, with a penetrating gaze. Like you knew me. Well, when I say you I mean this person who resembled you."

He chuckled softly. "It was me, little dragon. I was waiting for you. I didn't know how it would play out, but in one scenario, your parents could have let you start training at a young age."

"But it didn't happen that way."

"No, it didn't," he said, his voice calming me as always. "But that doesn't change the fact that this is your destiny. There is much yet to learn and discover while it unravels— all in due time. By the way, Phoenix, you fought like a pro that day, even if you don't feel you were all there."

"Wow," I said. "But...you look exactly the same age as you did then," I remarked.

"That's how it works, with us." His eyes flashed deep green again, for just a moment, and with that he winked, hugged me tightly, and disappeared.

I sighed. I wanted to know so much more—where they came from, where we were going, and if the "us" he referred to included me. "That's another tale for another time, dear Phoenix," Jin's voice echoed from afar...but still somehow near. I could hear the smile in it.

I sat on the beach next to my gorgeous hunk of a firefighter, staring out at the waves. There were two days left before we were to fly home. I rubbed SPF 15 on his back while he slept on his big turquoise beach towel. I got up and practiced my Half Moon stance, so I could say I did that at Half Moon Bay. I was cool like that.

I glanced down at Hammer, who had one eye open, and one corner of his mouth tilted upward in a smile. "You are so beautiful," he said, and went directly back to sleep.

I wouldn't have to make a choice between being with Hammer and Ninjitsu. I could do both. I had asked my trainer that. I had made sure that by saying I could be more than a wife, he meant I could add superhero in training to my skill set. He said even superheroes need support. I smiled at that. Truer words were never spoken. Hammer was meant to be on the path with me; this I knew for certain.

The waves beckoned, and I decided to go for a swim, just a little ways out. I wasn't sure how well my disappearing act worked in the water, so I wasn't brave enough to go into shark territory. Sharks were one thing this nanny, Ninja or not, would probably always fear. They come at you from below, where you can't see them. They have an unfair advantage and I wasn't going to be a mid-morning snack. I knew they fed early and late, so it wasn't really time, but I took no chances.

The water felt delicious—it was still quite cool, but the day had turned out to be abnormally hot, so I didn't care. Virtually weightless in the water, I thought back about the past week. After this latest episode I had come to, still on my bed, with the Ninja star in my hand. "Well, I'm quite sure I can't take this on the plane," I thought, chuckling. Hammer had been in the bathroom and asked me what was so funny, appearing in the doorway. Not wanting to take the time to explain what'd just happened, I shoved it under the bed, just in time. "Oh, just laughing at myself for falling asleep. At least I'm finished packing."

We had met with his parents, who I instantly fell in love with, and I believe the feeling was mutual. I'd gotten them a bathroom set: five candles, turquoise and white of different heights, on a decorative plate with all kinds of real seashells to be scattered around the candles, and some matching guest hand towels and washcloths, all meant for the bathroom. They gave me a card with a gift certificate for Bed, Bath and Beyond, and another for Ikea. The card said it was "just a little help to feather the nest," which I found incredibly sweet and generous. I couldn't believe I had people to call "Mom and Dad" again.

What happened next shocked even me, and these days my shock threshold was pretty high, with all that'd happened. We were preparing to leave, and I heard a siren coming up the driveway.

"What's that for?" I asked.

Everyone ignored me and went right on packing up and saying their goodbyes. Did no one else hear it? Was it a sign that I had I finally flipped my lid? Because after all that'd happened I really thought I might, at some point, just check out.

The siren got louder and louder. "Come on, guys, don't tell me you don't hear that?"

"Hear what, dear?" Hammer's mother said, feigning innocence. She gave me a hug, and a wink, and we were all but pushed out the door.

There in the driveway, sat the fire engine, decked out in all kinds of colored streamers. The back was painted with the words "Just engaged," and Tim sat in the driver's seat, in obvious amusement at the look on my face. He got out, and Hammer escorted me to the passenger's side. "Milady, your chariot awaits." I had absolutely no words, so I kissed him, got in, and Hammer drove our chariot all the way to the airport. After we dropped off Tim, of course, and after we went by, at my special request, Cameron and Courtney's house and waved. They were playing outside, all bundled up in their winter clothes, so it was perfect. I didn't know how they would get the fire engine back to the station, but for once I didn't care about the details, so I didn't ask. I just reveled in the magic of the moment.

Our flight had been uneventful and smooth. We'd had dinner the first night outside, by candlelight overlooking the water, and he had given me my ring. I would never forget what he said. "To the most amazing, resilient, beautiful woman I know. I will love you forever, no matter what, and will be by your side until such time as you no longer want me there, or until I pass on, whichever comes first." He slid the most beautiful ring on my finger—a diamond dolphin curled around a topaz stone. Perfect.

That night after dinner, we had left the doors of our room open to smell the salt air, and the white curtains swirled into the room. It was just like a scene from a movie, but I can't remember which one. It doesn't matter—we were the stars of our *own* movie. And Vin was right, our love scenes were hard to beat.

We had been blessed with clear skies for most of the week, visiting scores of cool places in San Francisco. I knew I'd be back here before long. Some places just called you until you went to them, you had no choice. Plus, I would definitely be visiting Sam when she moved down.

"Ouch!" I said, being forced out of my reverie of recent memories. I felt a sharp pain, and it wasn't from a shark. It was a cramp, and I immediately felt the need to get out of the water. I made my way toward the beach, struggling because the feeling was getting stronger. I felt like I was going to be sick, and wasn't sure it was from too much sun or from something I'd eaten—there was that Mexican dinner the night before and I had had a lot of fish on the trip. I started to sweat.

Lying on the sand, I looked over at Hammer. I saw him come toward me, and suddenly my vision blurred. I heard him yelling my name, and I was out.

I came to a while later but I wasn't sure how much, in the hospital. Actually, I thought, it must be the urgent care facility we had passed on the way into town.

"Natalie," Hammer said, rushing to my side from the chair he'd been sitting in.

"Hi," I said, my voice weak. "What happened?"

"Well, I carried you to the car, and you almost made it here before you had diarrhea," he said.

"Oh no. Oh no! It was the dinner, wasn't it?"

"I think so," he said. They ran some tests and I've been waiting impatiently to make sure you're alright."

"Jeez," I said. I looked around the room. The colors were very warm, unlike most hospital walls. At least I could focus again, my vision was fine. "Urgent Care?"

"Yes. I asked the wait staff as I was running by with you and they said it was the closest place open. How do you feel, babe?"

"Fine, now. I am sorry if I...pooped on you," I said.

"You didn't, don't worry. But your bathing suit... I'm afraid it will never be the same."

I laughed. He could really make me laugh. I considered this one of the keys to our happy relationship. "Oh, God." I looked under the blanket and sheets. Yep, I had a gown on but under that I was naked.

"And the rental car...well, we can fix that with some carpet cleaner and some handy wipes," he said.

"In the car? Oh, golly. Oh no. I didn't."

"Sorry."

I didn't have time to say what I was thinking, because the nurse came in.

"You're just fine, Natalie. We're fairly sure it was just what you ate last night."

"Good. That's what I thought. Usually I can handle spicy foods, but maybe not in combination with sun and swimming."

"Probably best to stay out of it until…tomorrow is when you leave?"

"Yes."

"Then I recommend you stay in bed for the rest of the day. You're free to go."

She left, and Hammer and I looked at each other. "Was I just ordered to stay in bed?"

"I believe you were."

"Well, I don't think I have a problem with that. I'm sure we can find something to do. Ya think?"

"I think you're right. I'm pretty sure."

"Oh yeah? How sure?"

"About…this sure." As he kissed me, he kept his eyes open and did that looking deep into my soul thing again, like he did that day we tipped the canoe. The warmth from his lips spread all the way through my body. And I knew he was right.

"My hero," I said. Even superheroes need…well, superheroes. ☺

Everything went back to normal after the trip—as normal as life could be for a ninja and a firefighter. I went back to my coffee day job, so that I could maintain my secret identity and pay the bills, but I wouldn't have as many bills, because Hammer and I were moving in together and

217

he was going to help me. He wasn't a pre-nup kind of guy, he was the type with a huge heart who recognized when someone he loved was in trouble and helped as much as he could. I wouldn't say I was in trouble. I just had other stuff to think about than paying bills right now...bigger stuff...superhero stuff.

We'd found a house on the water to rent. It was a fixer upper, but Hammer was excellent at household handyman tasks, and Sam said she needed something to do on the weekends to keep her mind off of the big change of moving to California, which was yet a month away.

I'd gone back to training and accepted the job of superhero in training with a sense of...cautious excitement. I knew I had so much to learn and couldn't wait to delve in. With increased knowledge came increased responsibility, so I knew to pace myself. So far, it was going well. I wouldn't be able to go into great detail. It was, after all, the art of stealth.

Hammer had gone back to being on call for the fire department because winter was the slow season for his other job, which meant I had more time with him, which was great. Things were a lot more normal now. We had settled into living together in my apartment until the beginning of February when the house would be ready. We packed, but took our time doing it, since we had a few weeks.

Hammer had found my Ninja star under the bed while packing a box of non-essential items and asked me about it. So I told him everything that had happened just before our trip.

He just sat there looking at me for a second. "Did you accept?"

"I did. I thought long and hard on our trip, and you know what? I couldn't *not* do it."

"Excellent. I wouldn't have it any other way."

"Do you mean it?"

"I do."

"I'm glad. Because I was going to tell you that I take both of my main duties in life equally seriously. I just want you to know that. I consider being your wife just as important a job as being the covert superhero in training known as Ninja Nanny."

"Well, I consider that a high compliment and I am honored to have a bodacious super heroine as my wife."

Oh, that's right, I almost forgot to mention—Hammer and I had gotten married on our trip to San Francisco. I always wanted to elope, and we did, on a beach there, with a justice of the peace who was happy to take his shoes off and join us in being barefoot. It was very romantic, as we'd written our own vows. To have a ceremony without all the bells and whistles felt right, and was a welcome relief from the chaos. I'd had enough bells, whistles, and sirens to last me quite a while, thank you very much.

We'd gone by the hospital where Bruce Lee was born, the Fire Department Museum, Fire Station #2—built in 1909, Alcatraz, Fisherman's Wharf, the Golden Gate Bridge and Golden Gate Heights Stairways, Haight Ashbury, and several other places on the trip, so the ceremony was completely spontaneous.

I wanted our friends and his family to be there, but obviously it didn't work out that way so we had a professional photographer take wedding photos on the beach and make a video of the ceremony so everyone could see later. Hammer and I wanted to make our wedding memorable and fun, so we went to a vintage clothing shop. We found old-fashioned clothes and purchased them the day before, giggling as we tried on costume after costume.

I chose a gown that looked like it was straight from the movie Grease. It swished when I walked. The bust was made of fuchsia-colored silk, and the rest of the dress was made of white silk taffeta. There were three matching fuchsia flowers hanging down the front. I also wore white beaded gloves, a matching faux pearl collar and bracelet, and of course an old-fashioned white lace veil.

Hammer looked handsome in his black and white, pinstriped suit. We actually found him a fuchsia-colored button up shirt and handkerchief that I artfully stuffed into the suit pocket. To top it off, he wore a black fedora. He looked amazing.

I couldn't begin to explain how much I loved this man—good-hearted through and through, and just simply knew things about me, without me having to spell them out to him, and he never ever called me Nat. In fact, he called me Natalia on occasion—said that's how he saw me, rare and exotic. He didn't even snore too loudly—just a low purr that blended well with those of the superhero cats.

Apparently, in rare cases, white picket fences come with ninja stars (and no actual picket fence). I'm very okay with that.

We found a guy playing his guitar on the beach and asked if he'd play for the ceremony for a small fee. He said he'd do it for free. We had him play Lullaby by the Dixie Chicks. As I heard the song, the beautiful lyrics ran through my mind:

How long do you want to be loved?
Is forever enough?
'Cause I'm never ever giving you up...

For a minute there on the beach, I swore I saw my parents, smiling at me. Then they disappeared.

Epilogue

Kiki and Claw nuzzled. Claw had gotten bigger and was almost as big as Kiki now. He would soon outgrow her and be her hot, buff younger man. I would have to get him some leather for next Halloween. Unless of course Kiki told me she wanted to be something totally different next year. I could somehow see that happening, but she still waited until I dozed off to talk to me. She was, after all, the cat of stealth.

The phone rang, and I ran to get it. Hammer was busy unpacking a box into our new living room.

I put the phone down gently, and walked towards him.

"Hammer, honey?" I said.

"Yeah, what's up?" he said, looking up from his box, Mr. Muscles in his t-shirt and jeans. The light from the window shined on his hair and he looked amazing. His eyes had gone from cheerful and content to concerned, because I didn't refer to him as "honey." Babe, sweetheart, and love, yes, but never honey.

"That was the clinic down in California. They apparently missed something in the test results. I'm pregnant..."

Dear Readers :

Thank you for being a part of NN's story and helping her make it through her initial superhero training! I wrote this while living in a basement apartment in the woods, with no internet, no television, and basically no distractions. Inspiration overtook me, there, and I could no longer ignore my muse who was knocking very loudly and persistently, leaving me no choice but to answer!

My launch pad was NaNoWriMo, or National Novel Writing Month (nanowrimo.org). If you're not familiar, the mighty goal is to reach the 50,000 word mark between November 1st and 30th. I highly recommend this as a way to join a movement with millions of other writers that, unless you join them at a write-in or other function, you don't ever see! But most importantly, you're racing against time. Writing in this fast fashion takes away the inner editor voice that stops so many writers in their tracks and impedes progress. I got to about 35,000 words, and called it a day. It took me until February to finish the first draft—then another five years, and three publishers, before I completed the final version you hold in your hands.

The life of this author is not exactly like Ninja Nanny's, but a sort of parallel universe version. I hope you've enjoyed the story and felt the magic of Natalie's adventurous world. This is an epic adventure in three parts, so the sequel and threequel will be out soon, as will a children's book.

Peace, love and roundhouse kicks!

Ninja Nanny

About the Author

Natalie Newport is a very busy kunoichi, or female ninja, fueled by caffeine. She's still trying to figure out the mysteries her cats conceal, and is determined to do this in the very near future. When not on a superhero mission, she practices and teaches yoga and martial arts religiously.

Natalie is an entrepreneur and editor, who leads workshops and classes that inspire women to be their superhero selves, their best selves, because the world needs it.

Find out more at: ninjananny.wordpress.com

Made in the USA
Charleston, SC
12 December 2011